"An eye-opening tale of dramatic events and richly diverse characters who discover that, with time, determination, and ahimsa, young people can solve real problems in the world."

—Cynthia Levinson, author of THE YOUNGEST MARCHER and WE'VE GOT A JOB

"Sprinkled with action as this story is, it is also packed with a wealth of interesting information and teachers and librarians will find much in this book to spur thoughtful discussions. Readers are also sure to discover parallels between the desegregation of schools in our nation and the attempt to integrate lower-caste children into the Indian education system. . . . A welcome addition to the growing body of South Asian literature for children in the United States."

—Padma Venkatraman, author of CLIMBING THE STAIRS and A TIME TO DANCE

"Kelkar gives us a front row seat at a critical moment in history with skill and emotion as we journey through India with Anjali, a feisty, inquisitive daughter of a freedom fighter who strives to stay true to Gandhi's philosophy of nonviolence, ahimsa, while tackling issues of colonialism, caste, women's rights and communal violence at the eve of the country's independence."

—N. H. Senzai, author of TICKET TO INDIA

AHIMSA

Supriya Kelkar

Tu BOOKS

an imprint of LEE & LOW BOOKS Inc.

NEW YORK

TU BOOKS,
an imprint of LEE & LOW BOOKS Inc.,
95 Madison Avenue, New York, NY 10016
leeandlow.com

Manufactured in the United States of America by
Worzalla Publishing Company, September 2017

Book design by Neil Swaab
Book production by The Kids at Our House
The text is set in Dolly Pro, Rukola, and Cowboy Junk

10 9 8 7 6 5 4 3 2 1
First Edition

Cataloging-in-Publication Data is on file with the Library of Congress

To my parents

CHAPTER 1

They wouldn't hang a ten-year-old girl, thought Anjali, clenching a small tin of black paint. She took care not to get any on the skirt of her saffron ghagra-choli woven with real gold thread. It was Anjali's Diwali present from last year, made from the most expensive fabric in the shop. She had picked it out herself. And she had managed to keep it as bright and crisp as the day she had gotten it, despite heavy monsoon rains that had drenched her little town in the middle of India.

"Hurry up," whispered her friend, Irfaan, as he glanced nervously around them. Perspiration beaded around his collar near the black thread of his taweez, the necklace whose locket contained Koran verses. Clad in a cool white pajama-kurta, he was more appropriately dressed for the muggy August weather than Anjali, but he couldn't stop sweating. "We can't get caught."

Getting caught vandalizing someone's property would lead to quite the punishment under normal circumstances, but Anjali was about to do far worse. She was about to vandalize a British officer's property. A British officer who was in charge of making sure the British Raj's orders were carried out in their town. A British officer who happened to be the former boss of Anjali's mother.

Only a week earlier, Anjali had stopped by the captain's office after school to catch a glimpse of her mother through the window, as she had often done for the past year since her mother became one of Captain Brent's secretaries. Anjali normally found her mother translating decrees and legal notices for Captain Brent, typing letter after letter on his behalf to their fellow townspeople, rejecting requests from families begging for mercy for their imprisoned freedom-fighter sons.

That day had looked like any other. She had found her mother hunched over the corner room desk, typing away, as Captain Brent lounged on his scarlet silk sofa under a faded oil painting of Queen Victoria. He was dictating to Anjali's mother in his harsh foreign accent, and Anjali couldn't help but stare.

The next day, her mother was out of a job.

Anjali still didn't know what had happened, only that her mother and father had fought, and that her great-uncle, Chachaji, who lived with her family, had never approved of her mother's job in the first place.

Anjali's mother had just become one of Captain Brent's secretaries when Chachaji moved in with them after a close call in one of the Hindu-Muslim communal riots that swept the city of Bombay in 1941. Chachaji was old *and* old-fashioned, and couldn't get past the fact that a woman was working outside the house.

But Anjali's father didn't mind that Ma worked. The extra money came in handy for feeding the extra mouth. And Anjali's mother was college educated, so why shouldn't she put her proficiency in typing and her fluency in English and five native Indian languages to use?

Anjali's mother hadn't mentioned Captain Brent all week, except to say she was relieved she didn't have to see him anymore. But there was something Ma *wasn't* saying. Had Captain Brent not paid her? Or had he hurt her? Anjali only knew one way to handle the situation: to hurt the captain back.

So when Irfaan got a half-empty container of paint from his father's newly painted dairy and asked Anjali what they should paint, she knew just how she'd do it. She and Irfaan would paint "Q"—short for "Quit India"—on the bungalow he worked out of. Maybe then Captain Brent and the other British officers would finally leave India for good.

Over the past few weeks, it seemed like all the British officers' houses and workplaces but Captain Brent's had been vandalized with a Q. He was definitely one of the more intimidating British officers, ordering everyone around regardless of their caste, acting like all Indians were Untouchable.

But what right did he have, when he had no caste?

What Anjali was about to do was terribly wrong and terribly dangerous. But she raised her paintbrush to the crumbling concrete anyway.

"Just do it before he sees us," hissed Irfaan, playing anxiously with his curls.

"I am," Anjali told him, irritated. "And relax. Everyone is still eating breakfast. The streets are empty. No one can see us."

Irfaan motioned behind them.

Across the street, a small girl coated in camel-colored

dust was crouched on the footpath near the empty paan stall, collecting a stray newspaper page that the paanwalla used to wrap his betel-leaf treats in. The girl's eyes met Anjali's, but Anjali didn't bother hiding the paintbrush.

"She's an Untouchable, Irfaan. She isn't going to say anything."

Untouchables were the lowest of the low in the ancient Hindu caste system, and were stuck doing the dirty jobs others in society wouldn't do, like cobbler work, leatherwork, clearing dead animals from the road, removing raw sewage from people's toilets, and cleaning garbage from the streets. And because they had no choice but to do these dirty jobs, everyone considered them dirty. Superstition said if you touched them, you would be cursed with bad luck or be unclean yourself, tainted by them.

And though her parents had never really mentioned their thoughts on the caste system, Anjali had heard such cautionary tales all her life from Chachaji, her neighbors, and her classmates.

Knowing there was no way this Untouchable girl would speak out of place and tell on her, Anjali turned back to the job at hand. She wasn't afraid of the girl. Or

Captain Brent. She was a member of the Brahmin caste, after all. Highborn.

Anjali's slim gold bangles jingled melodiously in the morning light as she raised her brush once again and finally painted a circle onto the chalky pillar, staining it a decaying black.

"There. Now you finish it," she whispered, handing the paintbrush over to Irfaan.

Perspiring heavily, even though he was in the cool shade of the tamarind tree behind them, Irfaan took the paintbrush and clumsily swatted it across the bottom of the circle. "Okay, now let's get out of here—"

"Quit India!" squealed Anjali, much louder than she had intended, then ducking back behind the pillar.

"What was that? Who said that?" bellowed a towering white man in his gravelly British accent.

Anjali and Irfaan peered around the pillar, keeping hidden, and watched as the man stormed out of the bungalow.

"Brent Sahib . . ." Irfaan was frozen in panic.

"Run!" shouted Anjali, dropping the small paint tin. Grabbing Irfaan by the arm, she raced through the streets, leaving behind the black Q on the outer wall of the bungalow's compound, but not before glancing back at the heavyset English officer seething at the defacement, his sunburned face turning even redder than usual.

The two friends sped around the bend, Captain Brent hot on their trail. They dodged a peacock and narrowly missed the street's paanwalla, a wrinkly old man who was on his way to open up his shop for business. They swerved past a white horse on the side of the road, decorated with pink feathers and a gold-and-pink saddle, ignoring the angry shouts of its owner. They ducked around barking street dogs, whose fur was thickly matted with dust. Anjali paused for a split second to pet a spotted puppy on the head, and then rounded another corner, down an alley that looked very different from the lane the bungalows stood on just a street away.

"What are you doing?" huffed Irfaan, trying to keep up.

"Shh." Anjali squeezed around the bend. Irfaan hesitantly followed her into a basti, a small cluster of a dozen tiny clay shacks with tin roofs. It was the Untouchables' basti.

The two of them plugged their noses, so as not to get a whiff of the hardened cow-dung cakes that were drying on the outer walls of the shacks to later be lit for fuel, and entered the maze of lanes.

It was hot and sticky in the narrow passageways, and they had to twist their bodies so as not to brush against the grime that was coating the impoverished dwellings. Anjali checked her ghagra. It was still unstained.

"Now look what you've gotten us into," Irfaan gasped. "We're stuck in some poor dung hole."

Putrid odors of rotting fish and open sewage floated around them as Anjali surveyed the area. Captain Brent was nowhere in sight. "At least Brent Sahib didn't catch us." She breathed a sigh of relief, forgetting that the subsequent inhalation would bring with it the stench of the underprivileged area. She gagged and hurriedly made her way out of the hiding spot, Irfaan right behind her as they ducked under some damp clothes hanging on a clothesline and came to the small clearing in front of the homes.

A few Untouchable children were starting a game of gilli danda near the exit to the main road. Anjali recognized the tallest one. It was Mohan, her family's toilet cleaner. Though he was thirteen, he didn't go to school. He couldn't. It just wasn't done in their town. Besides, even if he had lived near a missionary school that accepted every Indian student regardless of caste, he still wouldn't have gone to school. After all, he had to make a living. It was his job to remove the waste from their bungalow's outhouse every day. Mohan and his friends stopped hitting the gilli, the small cylindrical stick, with the danda, the larger stick, to stare at Anjali and Irfaan in wonder.

Anjali returned the stare, taking in the kids' sun-burned, crusty faces and their matted hair, no longer black but reddish-brown. When she was younger, Anjali had been envious of the basti kids' unique hair color. Her own hair was a boring, deep black, and it was so thick she kept it tied in two waist-long braids soaked in coconut oil. Then her father explained that the poor children's hair had turned reddish-brown from a lack of proper nutrition. Anjali never complained about her hair after that.

She glanced at the Untouchable children's dirty, tattered clothes, barely covering their scrawny frames. Her exquisite ghagra-choli, with its hand-embroidered floral border, must've looked unattainable to the kids.

The wobbling gilli rolled toward Anjali's feet.

"Don't touch it. Don't touch it or your chachaji will beat me!" shouted Mohan. "Please. He'll say we cursed you."

Anjali jumped back from the gilli. A slight wrinkle formed on her forehead, stretching her round red bindi into an oblong shape, as the children raced for their gilli, careful not to go near Anjali or Irfaan.

Yes, it would have been a bad day if she and Irfaan had been caught by Captain Brent. But for an Untouchable, every day was a bad day, Anjali thought as she turned away from them.

"Let's go home," she mumbled to Irfaan.

"I don't think so," muttered a voice from behind.

Anjali froze. It was Captain Brent.

He led Anjali and Irfaan by the elbows back down the street toward his pristine bungalow. Two servants were already busy bringing a can of white paint and brushes to the pillar, preparing to wipe out any evidence of Anjali's crime.

"Let us go." Anjali was trying to pry Captain Brent's pudgy fingers off her when she noticed a coin-sized smudge on her right arm: a blotch of black paint. Her stomach sank. She tried to scratch the paint off, but only a few shreds peeled away as Captain Brent led her up the stairs of his house, where her mother stood waiting, arms crossed.

"What are you doing here?" Anjali blurted, shocked but also relieved to see her mother. Even in frustration, Ma was radiant. A necklace of black and gold beads with a gold pendant dangled around her neck. Her flower-shaped diamond earrings sparkled. The stray strands of silver in her mother's otherwise midnight-black hair looked regal. She was wearing her peacock-colored sari, one of Anjali's favorites.

"I was coming back from meeting some friends in town. What are *you* doing out so early? And in your best ghagra-choli?" Anjali's mother asked.

"Painting the Q on my compound wall," replied Captain Brent before Anjali could respond, roughly releasing Irfaan and her from his grip. "I must say, Mrs. Joshi, I'm quite disappointed in you, if this is what your daughter is like. You're raising a common criminal."

Flustered, Anjali's mother turned to her. "Did you do it, Anjali?"

Anjali glanced at Irfaan. He was on the verge of tears. She had to get them out of this mess, so she steadied her voice and shook her head. "Of course not, Ma."

"You little liar," thundered Captain Brent. "I knew

you were a bad seed. You must be the most disobedient child in this whole bloody town. Perhaps in the entire British Empire."

Anjali wanted to giggle at Captain Brent's exaggeration. Imagine her being the most disobedient child in their little town of Navrangpur, much less the entire British Empire, which had controlled most of India for the last eighty years.

But Anjali's mother was not smiling. "This must be a misunderstanding—" she started, when a lady entered the compound. Wearing a simple cotton sari, deep lines of stress carved under her gray eyes, she approached Captain Brent with hands joined in a namaste.

"Here again." Captain Brent sighed. "As we tell you every day, Mrs. Mishra, we can't help you."

"But Sahib—"

"I will not write a letter of pardon for him," Captain Brent said loudly. "Your son burned down a municipal office."

"Please, Sahib." The woman's eyes glistened with tears. "Nobody died. He was overzealous in his love for India. He's just seventeen. Look. I brought you his picture. See? He's just a boy." She held up a tattered black-and-white image of her son, a tall teenager with a little mustache and big, light-colored eyes. "Please. They've set a date. They say he'll hang in the spring."

"Rules are rules, Mrs. Mishra," said Captain Brent as he led the woman off his porch. "Now off you go. I'm dealing with something important here, so have a good day, and please don't come back tomorrow."

Anjali watched her mother avoid eye contact with Mrs. Mishra. Did they know each other?

Captain Brent shook his head at the sight of the woman's tears trickling down her cheeks onto her son's photograph. He turned his attention back to Anjali. "Now where was I? Right. This uncivilized vandal you have raised."

Anjali's mother stood firm. "Please, Captain Brent. Is a splotch of paint on your wall more important than someone's life?"

Wait, is he actually considering hanging me? Anjali squeezed her mother's hand. "Ma . . ."

"How many times do we have to go over this? That boy is a criminal. He broke the law," Captain Brent said.

Anjali breathed a sigh of relief. They were talking about Mrs. Mishra's son, not her.

"There are rules in this land, thanks to us," Captain

Brent continued. "Those who disobey have to face the consequences. In this case, the consequence is hanging. That isn't my fault, Mrs. Joshi. That chap should have thought before setting fire to the property of the Raj."

Captain Brent turned back to Anjali. "You know something about destroying property too, don't you, little girl?"

Anjali held on even tighter to her mother.

Ma stared Captain Brent square in the eyes. "There are a hundred little girls in this town who could be mistaken for her. If my daughter says she didn't do it, she didn't do it."

Before Captain Brent could say anything, she took Irfaan by the hand and led Anjali and Irfaan off his property, running with the kids down the street, away from Captain Brent's bungalow.

Anjali was in complete shock. Her mother had defended her! Defended her lie.

Once they were a good distance from the captain's bungalow, they slowed down and Irfaan headed home. Anjali gave her mother a grateful hug, clutching Ma's waist. She could feel her mother's pulse as it raced from the morning's events, and wondered which of their hearts was beating faster.

"It's okay, Anjali," whispered Anjali's mother. There's nothing to be frightened of."

Anjali nodded, tucking a strand of hair behind her ear. Catching Ma's eyes, Anjali stopped abruptly, thinking of the smudge of black paint. While Mrs. Mishra was talking to Captain Brent, Anjali had tried to rub it off some more. Had Ma noticed it? Anjali quickly moved her arm behind her mother's back, squeezing her even tighter than before.

CHAPTER 2

*A*njali and her mother said little after that on the way home from Captain Brent's.

"What will Baba say when he hears about you fighting with Brent Sahib because of me?" asked Anjali anxiously as they entered Madhuban Colony, a neighborhood of pretty bungalows of varying pastel colors, and turned into house number forty-four, their home.

"Don't worry about that, Anjali," said her mother. "This isn't your fault."

Anjali looked down. If her mother knew this really was all her fault, she would be so disappointed in Anjali. They passed the custard concrete wall that surrounded her compound, and opened the iron gate to enter their property.

In the front yard, below the concrete porch that wrapped around the large pastel yellow one-story bungalow, stood Anjali's father. A tall man with thinning waves of hair splashed across his head, he crouched by their old metal hand pump to tend to the methi plants in the garden. While the rest of the foliage in the yard was a brilliant green thanks to the rains, the methi plants were dull, and what few little leaves were left on them were limp and covered with white specks of disease.

"Good morning, Baba," said Anjali, rushing past him straight and into the back corner of their yard.

Anjali loved it here. It was like her private zoo. The long, crimped leaves of the mango tree would sway lyrically in the summer breeze as if they were dancing. Families of monkeys would jump from tree to tree, playing with one another and fighting with the diving hawks that threatened their young. Tiny green lizards, striped squirrels, and an occasional slinky mongoose frolicked around the premises. But most importantly to Anjali, this was where Nandini lived.

Nandini was the family's cow. She lived under the shelter of a tiny shed consisting of three short concrete walls and four wooden pillars, one in each corner, that held up a clay shingled roof. She was all white, with a faint pinkish tint to her hind legs and underside. Two small off-white horns sat atop her head, and a wavy flap of skin rippled down, connecting her chin to her chest. Her belly was bloated, as she was at the beginning of her second pregnancy. She had lost a calf early on the first time around, when Anjali's parents had just gotten her last year, so Anjali was thrilled when Nandini became pregnant again. She just knew everything would work out this time, and hoped Nandini wasn't worried, either.

Nandini's big, beautiful black eyes seemed to understand everything Anjali said to her. When Anjali was happy, they sparkled. When Anjali was sad, Nandini's eyes would fill with tears. Anjali's mother always said the cow was the only animal that actually showed human emotions. And after spending the last year with Nandini, Anjali believed it.

Anjali ducked into the cow shed and wrapped her arms around Nandini's neck for a hug. She tried not to giggle as Nandini's warm breath tickled her ear and silently climbed up on the wooden milking stool to peer out of the tall window in the shed.

It was the perfect spot to listen to what was going on with her parents without being spotted.

In the front yard, Anjali's mother was gesturing wildly with her hands, her gold bangles furiously clanging against one another. It was something she did anytime she was excited about something. Or upset.

Anjali's chest tightened as her mother's voice grew loud enough for her to make out the words: "I told you, it's my choice. My decision."

Her father shook his head angrily. "You're not thinking clearly. It's irresponsible! It should be *our* decision!"

Anjali felt awful. Her parents had been fighting a lot the past week over her mother losing her job. Maybe money was getting tight with only Baba working. And now, after what Anjali had done, there was no way Captain Brent would ever give Ma her job back. Anjali poured some of the cow's water onto her arm and scratched at the paint splotch as hard as she could, finally erasing it from her arm. But not from her conscience.

There was just one thing left to do to fix all this.

Anjali was going to have to go see Captain Brent.

CHAPTER 3

*A*njali was back in front of Captain Brent's office for the second time that morning. But now she stood in line with a handful of Indians, waiting for her turn to see Captain Brent at the bungalow he worked out of. Every so often someone exited the house looking happy. But for the most part, people's brows were furrowed as they fanned themselves, and the thick, humid air wasn't helping anyone's mood.

As Anjali scanned their faces, a flash of gold and shimmering green caught her eye. She bent down. There, half caked in dirt, was a peacock feather. She picked it up and slid her fingers across the stringy feather. It was as soft as fur.

When Anjali was eight, she once had a particularly

rough day at school. Her teacher had punished her for not knowing an answer by whipping his ruler so harshly on Anjali's knuckles she thought her bones had broken. Anjali rushed out of the classroom, tears stinging her eyes. She rubbed her knuckles hard, and the first thing she saw was a glittering peacock feather on the ground. Something about its beauty made everything that happened earlier in class vanish. As she swiped the velvety feather over her swollen knuckles, she could swear they were healing.

Ever since then, anytime Anjali had a bad day, she would search for a peacock feather and just know things would get better. And now, finding one just outside Captain Brent's house, Anjali knew things were going to get better for her mother.

"Next," said a woman in a paisley-patterned silk sari as she glanced at a stack of papers. It was finally Anjali's turn.

Anjali tucked the feather into her waistband and nervously entered Captain Brent's office. He sat on his sofa, enjoying tea and biscuits with a handful of other Britishers—socialites and lesser officers.

When Captain Brent saw Anjali, he nearly choked. "You? Come to confess, have you?"

Anjali just stared apprehensively at him.

"Do we need a translator here?"

Anjali wanted to snap back at the obnoxious captain that of course they didn't. After all, she had just spoken English in front of him that morning. But she reminded herself she was there on a mission. To fix what she had messed up for her mother. To stop her parents from fighting. She took a deep breath and said slowly, "I understand English."

One of the socialites near the captain snickered.

She was laughing at Anjali's accent. Anjali's cheeks burned in embarrassment. She looked at the striking women in their imported dresses that ended just below the knees. Their eyes were as blue as the sea, a sharp contrast to Anjali's eyes, dark as monsoon rain clouds. Their blonde hair was either tied up in curls or hanging straight and low by their chins in odd, short bob cuts.

They looked so different from the Indian women Anjali normally saw. And she hated how little all of them were making her feel right now.

She took a deep breath, trying to sound strong. "Brent Sahib," she said respectfully, "I'm here to ask you to forgive my mother and give her back her job."

Captain Brent smiled. "Do you think my operations are at a stand-still without her? Look around." He pointed to the woman in the paisley sari, who was working at the typewriter. "Your mother has been replaced. You're all replaceable."

Anjali's stomach sank.

One of the English women giggled as she poured Captain Brent another cup of tea. "Really, William. You're awful," she whispered loud enough for Anjali to hear.

William? William Brent. Anjali had only known him as Captain Brent. As stern Captain Brent. Something to fear. Something to avoid. But here he was, "William Brent," sounding almost human. She had to give it one more try. Maybe she could appeal to this strange new human side of him.

"Please," Anjali said. "Think of our family. Isn't there something else she could do here?"

"Perhaps we do need a translator. Or maybe I just didn't make myself clear enough. The position has been filled. Now be on your way." With that, Captain Brent turned back to his conversation with the other Britishers. "Pests. All of them," he uttered between loud sips of tea.

Anjali frowned. "We're not the ones invading someone else's home like a cockroach."

Captain Brent's face burned, resembling one of those giant red bindis Anjali's neighbor, Lakshmi Auntie, liked to wear. "What did you say?" he snapped.

The new secretary quickly guided Anjali to the door. "It's time for the captain's next appointment."

Anjali tried to turn back. "But—"

"Next," the secretary called out to the ever-growing line of unhappy Indians waiting outside.

CHAPTER 4

*A*s a thunder rumbled outside, Mahatma Gandhi's shaky yet oddly strong voice quavered loudly from the static-filled radio inside the hall. "I know the British government will not be able to withhold freedom from us when we have made enough self-sacrifice." Sheets of rain tapped outside the house as he continued. "We must therefore purge ourselves of hatred. Speaking for myself, I can say that I have never felt any hatred."

Anjali badly wanted to go to the cow shed and be with Nandini after what had happened with Captain Brent. But her mother had spotted her in the yard and insisted she join Baba, Chachaji, and their maid

Jamuna inside their bungalow to listen to Gandhiji's "Quit India" speech from a few weeks earlier.

"As a matter of fact, I feel myself to be a greater friend of the British now than ever before. One reason is that they are today in distress. My very friendship therefore demands that I should try to save them from their mistakes . . ."

Anjali sat next to Jamuna, who was peeling soaked almonds into a bowl and sifting small stones and dirt out of some lentils by hand.

As Gandhi's speech ended, the radio announcer's voice spoke up amidst a burst of static. "Once again, that was Gandhiji's speech from earlier this month, eight August, 1942. Now Gandhiji is in prison, but we must not give up, my friends. As Gandhiji asked years ago, each family must give one member to help the cause. Together, we can do this."

Anjali stared at her parents, who were listening intently from their spots on the floor. Chachaji, on the other hand, was more interested in splitting apart the slices of a slimy orange.

"The British are growing weak," the radio announcer continued. "They cannot fight Germany and keep us under their rule at the same time. Now is the time to strike—but nonviolently, friends. Ahimsa always. So please send at least one person from your family to join the freedom movement."

Anjali had heard this plea before. In fact, the father of Anasuya, one of the girls in her class, had joined the movement when they were six. Nirmala, another classmate, lost her uncle to the movement when British police officers had fired into a crowd of protestors. Anjali scooted closer to Baba. Thank goodness he hadn't joined.

The radio announcer continued. "The more of us there are, the louder our collective voice will be. Jai Hind."

"Jai Hind," replied Anjali's father, repeating the salute to India. Anjali's mother did the same.

"What Jai Hind?" asked Chachaji gruffly as he dipped small pieces of his orange into a mix of salt and pepper, filling the room with the sour scent of citrus. "The Indian National Congress passed that resolution demanding immediate independence a month ago, and nothing has happened."

"That's why Gandhiji asked us to join the Quit

India movement, Chachaji," answered Anjali's father. "Together we can make a difference. Massive civil disobedience can have results."

"Your Gandhi was arrested the day after he made this speech. Do you see any results?" Chachaji spat a slimy orange seed into his coarse, lined palm. "If you ask me, we're better off with the Brits here. Look outside. Good roads, nice railways, a postal system . . ."

"That is all good and well, Chachaji, but what about unfair taxes on salt?" retorted Anjali's mother. "So many people couldn't afford the salt they fell ill from the lack of nutrients. Or what they have done to our cotton industry? We are a land rich in cotton, but instead of villagers spinning it, it's being processed overseas and the cloth sold back to us at unfair rates. I was blindly following orders when I worked for Captain Brent. Helping all these injustices continue. Not stopping to wonder if what I was doing was fair or even nice. But I was wrong. No group of people should be forced to live under the imposed will of another."

Anjali beamed. Her mother was so eloquent that nobody could win a verbal match against her, especially not a wrinkly relic like Chachaji.

"Hmph," snorted Chachaji. "In my day, women never

dared to be so disrespectful. It's a good thing you finally got some sense and quit that job."

A pit grew in Anjali's belly as she thought of Captain Brent smirking at her. *Quit? Ma quit her job?*

"Your place is in the home," Chachaji continued.

"Not anymore. Times are changing, Chachaji. Perhaps you should too," Anjali's mother replied.

Chachaji's lip quivered as he turned to Baba. "Are you going to let her speak to me that way?"

Ma looked at Baba. "Are you going to let *him* speak to *me* that way? I have enough on my mind, with Captain Brent accusing Anjali of vandalism—"

Anjali couldn't take it anymore. "Everybody, stop!" she shouted. "Please. I have to tell you something."

"What is it, Anju?" Her mother using her nickname made Anjali feel even guiltier.

Anjali took a breath. "I painted the Q," she said softly.

Her mother's face dropped. "You what?"

"I did it. I painted the Q on Brent Sahib's compound."

"I knew she was up to no good," grumbled Chachaji.

"Why?" Ma's voice was stern.

Anjali shrugged. "Because I thought Captain Brent wasn't treating you well. If he hurt you, I wanted to hurt him back. Irfaan had some paint, and I just thought—I thought we should tell Captain Brent to quit India. I thought that's what you and Baba wanted. And now you're not working, and I don't know why. And Baba is mad. And you and Chachaji are fighting. And we won't have extra money, and I won't get any new ghagra-cholis." Anjali fought back her tears. "Can you ever forgive me?"

Ma's face softened as she knelt next to Anjali and stroked her hair. "Anjali, do you know what 'Quit India' means?"

Anjali nodded. "The Brits are not Brahmins, but they think they're better than all of us. It's time to remind them of their place."

"No. It has nothing to do with some people being better than others. Irfaan isn't a Brahmin. But you think of him as your brother."

"That's different," replied Anjali. "Muslims don't have castes."

"Neither do the British. Gandhiji thinks of them as our brothers. Our equals. Quit India is a movement of civil disobedience," said her father.

"Like Henry David Thoreau's essay," Anjali said, remembering the piece her mother had told her about earlier that year.

"Yes, Gandhiji was influenced by Thoreau, but Gandhiji's practice of civil disobedience is peaceful," explained her mother. "It's based on ahimsa."

"That's right," said Anjali's father. "Nonviolence. It means it's time to put all our efforts into the highest of gears. But we must never hurt someone in the process. Lying, destroying someone else's property, those are things that can hurt others."

"Gandhiji says the British can stay in our country, but as brothers, not rulers, understand?" asked Anjali's mother.

"You want Brent Sahib to stay? He is mean to everyone. He treats us like we're all Untouchables. He thinks he's better than all of us."

"I think it's time to tell her," Baba said.

Anjali frowned. "Tell me what?"

"Here, eat your almonds," Ma said, handing her the small steel bowl with five nuts Jamuna had just peeled. "It's good for the brain."

"My brain is fine." Anjali pushed the almonds away. "Tell me what?"

Chachaji chomped loudly on the discarded almonds.

"We didn't help out with the freedom fight as we should have earlier. We were busy, raising you, working, earning a living . . . but now, well, with Gandhiji and so many of our leaders imprisoned by the British, we decided we must give one family member to the free-dom fight."

Anjali's face flushed. They must have decided this because her mother was no longer working. She could be at home to watch Anjali, and her father could go march and protest and get arrested—and possibly be hanged. Now she would be just like her classmate Anasuya, always wondering where her father was and if he was all right.

She couldn't imagine life without Baba. Who would help her fly her mango-colored kite on the terrace and cut Irfaan's pink one in the kite battles? Who would catch the flying cockroaches that entered the house during the rains and gently put them outside with-out hurting a wing on them? Who would play carom with her on Sunday afternoons for hours, despite the eventual swollen, painful fingers the game brought? A hundred thoughts and memories flooded Anjali's face. "You can't go, Baba."

"He's not going," said Ma.

Anjali breathed easier.

Ma cleared her throat. "I am."

CHAPTER 5

*A*njali woke with the sun. It wasn't the sounds of the noisy roosters, peacocks, and monkeys outside that woke her up. It wasn't the light knocking of the rain on her windows. It was the sound of her belly rumbling because she had gone to sleep without eating the night before.

Brushing away the memory of her mother's announcement, Anjali changed into her sky-blue salwar kameez, her school uniform, consisting of a long-sleeved tunic and pants, and then draped the navy-blue sash over her neck.

Anjali's mother had hugged her tightly right before bed. "I'm not going away forever, Anju. Just think of this as my new day job. Like your father is a professor, I'm a freedom fighter."

Ma? A freedom fighter? It makes no sense.

Anjali twisted her hair into two braids. Usually her mother did this for her when she was running late. Anjali knew how to braid her own hair, but she loved when her mother ran her fingers on Anjali's scalp, rubbing coconut oil into it to keep the roots of her hair nourished. Now she wouldn't be able to ask her mother for help because Ma left too early in the morning. Wiping away the tears welling in her eyes, Anjali looped the braids on either side of her head, tied them with a navy-blue bow, as per school dress code, and exited her room.

Chachaji was in the hall reading the morning paper. Anjali quickly bowed down in a respectful pranaam before him, grazing her right hand on the top of his foot before bringing her hand to her head, but he didn't look up from behind his paper.

"What nonsense," was the only thing Chachaji had muttered yesterday upon hearing her mother's news. Rather than try to stop Ma, Anjali's cantankerous old great-uncle had huffily made his way to his bedroom for an early afternoon nap.

Anjali had turned to her father. "Why didn't I have a say in this?"

"This was a decision for Ma and me to make, Anju, not you," her father had told her. "And it didn't come out of nowhere. We have been discussing this for months now. We always knew one of us would be going."

"And your father has to work to support us, so he cannot join the fight full-time. This is the only way," her mother had added.

They'd known about it for months? How could they have not said a word?

As Anjali made her way into the kitchen, she found herself alone with Jamuna, who was toiling away over breakfast, dressed in her loudly patterned, multicolored sari, the free end tucked into her petite waistband. Sitting on the rectangular wooden platform three inches off the ground, Jamuna took a pan off the kerosene stove that sat on the floor. She spooned some poha—flattened rice with potatoes, onions, cilantro, and shredded coconut—onto a steel plate.

"There you are, Anjali. I soaked your almonds. Your breakfast is getting cold," she said, setting the steaming plate down.

Anjali stared at the stainless steel dish of home-made yogurt by her plate, engraved with her mother's name and the year 1931, the year her parents got married. Chachaji's wife had given Anjali's mother several of these dishes as a wedding present shortly after she and Chachaji had arranged the marriage with Ma's parents. A little glass jar nearby held wedges of lime pickle with its sweet and spicy syrup.

"Start. Your father is already outside," Jamuna said as she served Anjali.

Anjali peeked out the window. Sure enough, as the last few drops of rain fell from the sky, her father was in the backyard, making a puckering noise with his full lips and scattering a handful of rice and grains on the ground. A few tiny brown sparrows and cooing pigeons, who had been waiting patiently for the rain to stop, descended on the yard, happily gobbling up the food. Anjali's father had a policy that you had to take care of others before you took care of yourself. He insisted on feeding the birds and the street dogs every morning before allowing himself and his family to eat.

"Jamuna, Ma won't really join the freedom fight, will she?" Anjali asked in between bites.

"Anjali, eat your breakfast," Jamuna replied.

Anjali stopped chewing. She knew her low-caste maid wasn't in any position to talk her mother out of her decision, but she did think Jamuna would at least express some sympathy.

"Jamuna, did you know about Ma's and Baba's decision?" she asked.

"Hurry up, Anjali, or you'll be late to school."

As it turned out, Anjali was late. She rounded a large peepal tree and ducked into the classroom fifteen minutes after school had started. Pragati, the little one-room schoolhouse on a hill, whose name meant "progress," was just down the street from Captain Brent's office.

"Anjali, your tardiness will not be accepted next time," said Masterji, their teacher, who tightly held a wooden ruler used more for punishments than for measuring. "It is disrespectful to me and the other students." His mustache fluttered, briefly showing his teeth, stained red from eating too much betel leaf.

"Yes, Masterji," said Anjali, hoping to avoid the sting of the ruler on her knuckles.

As she took her seat behind Irfaan, Anjali felt the other students watching her. Some of them giggled. She saw Anasuya and Nirmala and felt a pang of guilt. Anjali had always considered herself so lucky compared to them because their family members had joined the freedom fight and hers hadn't. Now they were all in the same boat.

One of her classmates was still snickering. Suman. Anjali should have known. She was their neighbor Lakshmi Auntie's daughter and one of the most competitive girls Anjali knew, always determined to rank at the top of the class, and usually succeeding. Anjali wanted to turn around and snap at Suman that she could stop giggling now, that Anjali was clearly not going to endanger Suman's ranking in class. But Anjali decided it wasn't worth getting in trouble with Masterji and bit her tongue.

Masterji was now writing math problems on the chalkboard. Anjali furrowed her brow, trying to forget about her parents and Chachaji and Jamuna and Suman and focus. But it was no use. How could she focus on math when her whole world was changing?

When school let out, Anjali headed up the street to Captain Brent's. She didn't know why she went or what she was looking for, but she had to go. Mrs. Mishra was standing outside, but Captain Brent was nowhere in sight. Nor was the Q Anjali and Irfaan had painted. It was as if they had never touched the wall of his compound.

Dejected, Anjali had turned for home when she saw Anasuya passing by with her little metal tiffin container down a dirt road to the side. Anjali didn't know why, but she had to follow her. She had to see the kind of life Anasuya led as the child of a freedom fighter. She had to see what her own future was going to look like.

Keeping her distance, Anjali trailed behind her classmate. Anasuya was dressed in her school uniform today, but the one time Anjali had seen her outside of class, at the fair that came to town every winter, Anjali had been shocked. All the other kids had worn their most vibrant clothes, and many of them had tiny pieces of shiny mirrors sewn into the fabric that glistened when they caught the reflection of a lantern's flickering flame. It was a fair, after all. A celebration. But not Anasuya. She was dressed in a boring white cotton ghagra-choli. White was usually reserved for funerals, but many of the freedom fighters wore it. The material had seemed coarse and stiff compared to the soft, flowing ghagra-choli Anjali had been wearing that day with embroidered blue sleeves on the choli and diamond-shaped mirrors adorning the maroon-and-blue ghagra, the ankle-length skirt.

Anjali never figured out why Anasuya dressed so plainly. But it made her boring classmate seem even more boring, and worse, a little sad.

Anasuya rounded the corner near a blossoming bougainvillea vine spilling magenta petals over the cracked concrete wall that surrounded the buildings in this neighborhood. There were no bungalows here like where Anjali lived. Just a bunch of two-story buildings that stood awfully close together, housing several families inside.

Even though she and Anasuya were both Brahmin, their living conditions were very different. Anasuya's father had worked as a journalist for the newspaper. The pay was clearly not as much as Baba's college job.

Dodging a scowling monkey who was eating a guava while snarling at passersby, Anasuya entered an open gate and headed toward an off-white building. She paused briefly to talk to her mother, a woman in an oil-stained sari, who was crouched in the yard, untying a cotton sack full of dried red chili peppers. And then Anasuya went inside.

Making sure Anasuya was far enough ahead to not see her, Anjali snuck through the gate and hid behind a cluster of sweet lime trees near the property entrance. They were full of overripe fruit, attracting all sorts of bugs and noisy black crows.

She watched the building before her for any sign of Anasuya. Finally her classmate exited the building, now dressed in a plain white ghagra-choli. *Or rather, it once was white*, thought Anjali, feeling bad for Anasuya. Months of wear and the town's dust had turned the dress a dingy, dirty-looking shade of beige.

Is this what my life is going to be like? Will my family lose our bungalow and be forced to live in a tiny house? Will we become poor? Anjali shook her head, reminding herself that Baba was still working at the college, that they could afford their house. They could afford their nice clothes.

Anasuya slowly went up to her mother, who was now standing before a large, cylindrical stone mortar, pounding the peppers into powder with a four-foot-tall wooden pestle. With Anasuya's father always gone, Anasuya's mother had started making food, including labor-intensive masalas, to sell to other households.

It must be exhausting, Anjali thought as she watched Anasuya's mother brush her hair out of her face and arduously struggle with the pestle, coughing from the peppery dust, and wiping her burning eyes. Anasuya said something to her that Anjali couldn't hear. Anasuya's mother exploded. She banged the pestle on the edge of the mortar and screamed at her daughter. Anjali could only catch bits here and there like, "You know we can't afford that!" and "Your father has no idea what he has done to us. We are ruined!"

Tears filled Anasuya's eyes. She looked away from her mother. Right into Anjali's eyes.

Caught, Anjali stepped out from behind the trees and made a dash for the gate. She ran down the uneven road, turned the corner, and almost collided with Anasuya. She must have come out the back alley.

"What are you doing here?" Anasuya asked, her cheeks red with embarrassment and anger.

"Nothing— I—"

"Are you spying on me? Came to see what poor little Anasuya's life is like?"

Anjali shook her head. She couldn't look Anasuya in the eyes. "I just . . . I just wanted to know what it was like," she mumbled.

"Did you see enough?" Anasuya asked angrily. "I showed my mother that I dropped my tiffin container at lunch, and the lid got so dented it can no longer close. And she screamed at me at the top of her lungs. Because thanks to my father giving up his job, we can't afford a new container."

"I'm sorry," Anjali said, feeling bad she was worrying about the changes in her comfortable life when Anasuya's family couldn't even afford a new container for her school lunches. "My mother, she's joined the freedom movement."

Anasuya laughed.

This was not the reaction Anjali was expecting.

"Your mother? Captain Brent's secretary?"

Anjali's face heated up. "She doesn't work for him anymore."

"You are going to wear khadi?" Anasuya laughed even harder. "I can't wait to see Suman's face."

CHAPTER 6

What was khadi? What did Suman have to do with any of this? Anjali didn't know but she didn't want to be laughed at any longer, so she raced all the way back to her neighborhood.

As she turned down the road toward her bungalow, she saw her neighbor Suman with her parents, exiting their house. Suman was dressed in an indigo-and-yellow ghagra-choli with exquisite gold zari borders. It was more beautiful than anything Anjali owned. Before she could look at it any longer, Suman and her parents rounded the corner to the next street, disappearing from her sight.

Anjali opened her gate, right next door to Suman's gate, and found Ma pacing anxiously in the front yard.

"There you are, Anjali. We have been waiting for you."

"What's going on?" Anjali asked, still trying to make sense of Anasuya's cryptic words.

"We're going to begin joining our countrymen in their fight by doing something . . . special," Ma said, "and we want you to take part."

Had her parents changed their mind about the vandalism? Would they be painting the letter Q on the fences surrounding more British officers' homes? Or making "Quit India" signs for a protest? Anjali couldn't imagine what her parents had in mind and was a little nervous to find out.

She entered their compound to see a pile of her mother's elegant saris and Baba's shirts and pants lying on a cot on the porch. "What is going on?" she asked again, bewildered.

She thought of Mohan and the other Untouchable children's tattered clothing. Were they donating their old clothes? In the past Baba had given Mohan a couple of his old shirts, but never Ma's saris. And besides, the clothes on the porch did not look old. She recognized the new pajama-kurta her father had gotten for his birthday which he had proudly worn every Friday to teach at the college. And her mother was holding her wedding sari. Her gorgeous red sari with gold embroidery.

Ma put her arm around Anjali and gently led her up the porch stairs. "Run and get every one of your ghagra-cholis that we bought from the city."

"I don't understand," said Anjali, catching a sharp whiff of kerosene as she passed the cot.

"Just trust me."

Anjali ran to her room. She opened the wooden armoire, the musty scent of mothballs filling the air, slid aside her other school uniform and a couple thin cotton ghagra-cholis she wore at home and slept in, and pulled out her exquisite dresses. They were magenta, purple, cucumber green, crimson, deep blue—the most gorgeous, vibrant shades Anjali had seen. *Even Suman probably doesn't have this many different colors to choose from. But what does Ma want with them?*

She eyed the saffron ghagra-choli she had worn the day before. Her beautiful Diwali present. Was Ma going to make her donate all her clothes to the poor? Anjali couldn't dream of parting with her favorite outfit, so she folded it up and tucked it under her mattress, deep in the middle of her bed so no one would find it.

She then gathered the rest of her dresses in her arms

and ran out to the yard where Ma now stood holding her saris and Baba's clothes. Anjali was in such a hurry to find out what was going on, she had forgotten her sandals, so the occasional stone in the damp earth pricked her feet.

"Good," Anjali's mother said, leading her out the front gate. Her mother dropped the clothes to the ground. "Now throw them on the pile."

Anjali stared at her parents' expensive clothes lying in the dirt by the side of the road and clutched her ghagra-cholis tightly. "How can we put our clothes on the ground?" she asked, looking at Suman's gate next door for any sign of her. People chewing paan spat red saliva out on the road. Why would her mother want their clothes near that filth?

"These clothes were made with cotton from India, but the British took the raw cotton, spun it in England, and sold it back to us as finished cloth at very high rates," her mother explained. "The first step to a free India is to only buy homespun clothes and be self-sufficient. So we must get rid of these garments that enslave us."

Anjali shook her head, confused by everything coming out of her mother's mouth. She thought about the simple clothing Anasuya had started wearing after her father joined the freedom movement. She had assumed that Anasuya's family no longer had enough money to buy fancy ghagra-cholis. But this was by choice? *Is this what it's like to be the daughter of a freedom fighter? Is this what Anasuya was laughing about?*

"I know . . . I thought I could never do it a few years ago when Gandhiji asked. The sari I wore at my wedding, the saris my mother gave me—they're all imported; how could I part with them? But now I know I must."

"Don't worry," added Anjali's father, exiting the gate. "You still have your uniforms and home clothes, and we'll get other clothes for you." He stopped when he saw the garments on the ground. "Why have you thrown them into the dirt? Now how will we give them to the poor?"

"I told you. If someone else uses the clothes, there will still be people walking around in foreign-spun clothes. The British will have won." Without another word, Ma lit a match and dropped it into the clothes. With a resounding *whoosh*, flames erupted, ravaging the finely tailored clothes.

"What are you doing?" Anjali shrieked. She stood

frozen in shock as her mother's gorgeous wedding sari went up in flames.

"What have you done?" asked Baba, trying to kick down the flames.

But it was too late.

Ma squeezed Baba's hand. "I'm sorry. It's the only way. Besides, I had already doused my clothes in kerosene."

Anjali's father sighed as neighbors and strangers passed by. He did not look happy, but he didn't say another word. There was clearly no stopping Ma.

Is this what he was arguing with Ma about yesterday?

Ma turned to Anjali. "It's your turn."

Anjali shook her head, clinging to the clothes. Her fingers ran over each deliberate bump and stitch in the embroidery as she wished desperately that a gray cloud from above would cry down some tears, putting the fire out.

"You can do it, Anjali. Jai Hind," chanted her mother.

People were stopping to watch the spectacle now. Anjali caught the eye of a neighbor, widowed Veena Auntie. Everyone was staring. Anjali had never seen such determination in Ma's eyes.

"Come on, Anju! Now!"

Anjali's hands went limp. Her clothes tumbled lifelessly into the fire. The blaze suddenly grew larger, roaring as it devoured Anjali's prized dresses.

Ma beamed, the reflection of the flames fluttering in her eyes. The light of the fire tinged her face an unnatural orange. Anjali's face grew hot, but not from the heat of the bonfire. Her eyes began to sting. Her ears started to burn. She ran away from her parents, away from the spiraling cloud of dusky smoke spewing from the fire. She ignored the sharp pokes of the rocky soil on her unprotected feet and, anklets jingling feverishly, headed straight to her cow shed.

Anjali collapsed in the stall, her arms around Nandini's neck. As she petted the stiff, short white hairs on the gentle cow's body, Anjali broke down. Tears flooded from her eyes, rendering her face a sticky mess. Tears also filled Nandini's eyes. Concerned, the cow nuzzled Anjali, rubbing her chin on Anjali's clammy face.

Anjali sobbed, her whole body shaking, as the nauseating stench of burning clothes drifted past her in the warm afternoon air.

CHAPTER 7

The next morning, Anjali awoke, positive she could still smell the earthy odor of burning clothes in her hair. She had asked Jamuna for two buckets of hot water and two buckets of cold water for her shower, instead of the one bucket of each she normally used. Jamuna had complained that now she would have to go pump more water in order to have enough to cook with, but gave in. Anjali crouched in the shower, mixing the hot and cold buckets into empty buckets, creating the perfect temperature as she scrubbed at her hair. With so much of the shikakai rinse that Jamuna had boiled for her, her hair *had* to be clean. But she just couldn't get the sickening stench out of her mind.

They were gone. All her beautiful, expensive clothes

were gone in a puff of smoke. All that was left were her two school uniforms and a couple old, faded cotton ghagra-cholis she wore at home and slept in. Now she would look just like Anasuya, in plain, boring, ugly clothes. What would Suman think? Anjali's competitive neighbor would have that smug smirk plastered on her face at Diwali and other holidays, when she would have the most gorgeous clothes on the whole street. And Anjali would be dressed in white like a person in mourning.

How fitting, Anjali thought. After all, her old life was now just a memory, dead and gone forever.

If joining the movement was her mother's decision, she should have just burned her own clothes. Anjali hadn't agreed to join.

But Anjali certainly didn't approve of Captain Brent and the British ordering everyone around, either. Her brow furrowed as she dried her hair with a fraying cotton cloth, braided it, and changed into her school uniform.

Chachaji was in the hall, reading the paper. Anjali rushed over the slate tiles, hoping she wouldn't have to see her parents, and bowed down in respect to Chachaji. She spotted her father outside, feeding the birds, and sat down at the table, where she spooned bite after bite of the steaming breakfast into her mouth, trying to ignore how numbingly hot the poha was on her tongue. She had nothing to say to her parents after yesterday's events, and had spent most of the evening giving them the cold shoulder, responding with one-word sentences when they tried to talk to her. And now she wanted to get to school without having to talk to them again.

Chachaji always said Anjali's parents were too lenient with her. That no other parents would tolerate their child sulking when he or she was upset. Anjali didn't think this made her parents too easy; she thought it meant they were so close she could show her true self to them. Irfaan never, ever spoke back to his father. He always appeared shocked when Anjali contested her own parents. In fact, none of her classmates spoke back to their parents. That was just how things were. Your parents were your elders. They were always right, and you always listened to them. But how could burning clothes be right? They didn't even donate them to Jamuna or some other poor person. They just set them on fire and erased them. What a waste.

Anjali was swallowing the last bite when her father entered the kitchen. He handed Anjali's schoolbooks to her. "I'm glad to see you're eating, Anju," he said. "Ma is at an early morning meeting but should be back soon."

A meeting. It all made sense now. Every morning the week before announcing that she was joining the freedom fight, her mother would walk Anjali to school and then continue to walk down the street instead of turning back to their bungalow. She had told Anjali she was going to meet some friends now that she had free time, but she had really been going to secret freedom fighter meetings every morning since she quit working for Captain Brent. It must have been why she was passing Captain Brent's bungalow when he had caught Anjali painting the Q last weekend.

Baba put his hand on Anjali's shoulder. "She wanted to walk you to school."

Anjali abruptly got to her feet. "I'm late. I'll see her after school."

And with that, Anjali rushed out the door to class.

Anjali sat at the small school bench behind Irfaan, looking at the other girls in her class. Nirmala, taller than even the boys; Mangala with her sunburned nose; Suman, who was looking more and more beautiful by the day, like the film star Leela Chitnis . . . Anjali wondered what they would wear in a few months at Diwali. And what they would think of her having to wear ugly homespun cotton clothes like Anasuya.

She bit her lip, trying to forget about her dresses and focus on today's lesson. It was poetry, her least favorite subject. Masterji was in the middle of reading an epic poem by the freedom fighter Subhadra Kumari Chauhan, about the exploits of the Queen of Jhansi.

> "The fires of the revolution began as a spark in
>   the palace.
> The commoners turned it into raging flames.
> The flames of freedom grew from the souls of
>   the people and spread from city to city.
> From the folk singers of Bundelkhand, we
>   heard the courageous tale of the warrior
>   woman, who fought like a man against the
>   British invaders.
> That was who the Rani of Jhansi was."

Masterji paused, looking up from the poem. "Subhadra Kumari Chauhan is currently in prison for protesting the British. Think of her bravery as you think of the Rani of Jhansi's bravery," he added, before going back to the seemingly never-ending poem.

Anjali scribbled verse after verse of the poem down in her notebook. She swung her legs under the old wooden bench, accidentally smacking Irfaan's bottom in the bench ahead with her foot. He turned to scowl at her.

"Sorry," she said, stifling her laughter.

"Anjali? Did you say something?" asked the teacher.

"Sorry, Masterji," said Anjali, glancing nervously at the ruler in his hand. She looked apologetically at her teacher, trying to hide the dislike she felt for him.

The teacher nodded, looking just beyond the classroom door into the hall. "Good. That's it for poetry for today. We have a special guest who is going to teach you about a charkha."

Anjali turned as the door opened. And then her face dropped.

It was her mother. She was dressed in a white cotton sari Anjali had never seen before. It must have been from that homespun shop in the business district.

Anjali stared at its rough fibers. It was so plain compared to the elaborate clothing her mother used to wear. There was just one tiny indigo stripe decorating the sari's border.

Ma gave Anjali a small smile as she brought a two-inch-tall wooden box to Masterji's desk.

Anjali turned away. She wasn't going to make eye contact with her mother, let alone speak to her after what she had done yesterday. Why was she at Anjali's school? Was this part of her job in the freedom movement?

"Good afternoon, class," said Anjali's mother, opening the hinged box like a book and showing them what was inside. "This is a charkha—a spinning wheel."

When her mother wasn't looking at her, Anjali glanced at the low-lying wooden box. Now opened flat, it was almost three feet long. Inside it were two flat wheels, one large and one small, side by side on the floor of the right side of the box. This was what used to be the bottom of the box when it was closed. Fragile strings of cotton wound around the wheels crossing over to the left side of the box—what used to be the lid when it was closed—and wrapped around a sharp metal spindle that stuck out on that side.

"Gandhiji uses the charkha to spin Indian cotton into thread, which will then be made into khadi, homespun clothes."

Khadi. The word Anasuya had used. It was what the ugly cotton sari Ma was wearing was called. Anjali gave a small sideways glance at Anasuya, who was smirking.

Anjali's mother must have gotten that spinning wheel at her meeting that morning. What had she been doing all last week at her meetings? Maybe they had taught her how to use it then. Or maybe she was protesting the British like other freedom fighters did. Anjali had no idea and had no interest in finding out. She was still too upset with her mother.

"This is my starter spool," said Anjali's mother, pointing to the strings of yarn that were wrapped around the spindle. She took a handful of raw, fluffy cotton with her left hand, and strung it to the starter yarn as she turned a knob on the large wheel with her right hand. Within seconds, the puff of cotton grew smaller as it was spun into twisty thread. But her mother's hands kept slipping. She was clearly new to spinning.

Anjali's mother wiped the sweat from her forehead as she tried to untangle the knots. "It's so hot in here." She laughed nervously. "Sorry. I've been learning to spin for a week now. It normally doesn't act up like this."

Anjali watched as the thread kept tangling up and her mother got frustrated. Maybe she would realize she was bad at this freedom fighter thing and quit this job too.

But Ma didn't give up. "When I was young, we used to have class out under a large peepal tree in the summer months. Just like the one you have outside." She struggled with the strands that were fanning out every which way. "You know why?" The class sat silently, watching the awkward display in front of them. "It is the sacred tree where Buddha meditated and became enlightened. Our teacher used to say maybe it would help us get enlightened too. Or at least a little smarter." She fumbled with more cotton, spinning it unevenly.

Anjali thought about her clothes disappearing into the blaze yesterday. "Looks like my uniform is safe," she muttered.

Her mother gave her a warning glance.

"I was afraid you'd be so good at using the charkha you would burn my uniform so that you could make a homespun one. But looks like you won't be able to."

A flash of hurt sparked in her mother's eyes, and Anjali immediately regretted her words. Some of her classmates giggled, but Masterji smacked Anjali's knuckles with his heavy ruler.

She fought back tears as she rubbed her hand, her knuckles throbbing. Ma rushed to her side, but Anjali pulled back. "I'm fine," she lied, squeezing her knuckles to try to dull the pain.

"Are you sure?" Ma asked.

Suman stifled a laugh from the back.

"I said it's fine," Anjali snapped.

"Okay . . ." Her mother nodded, returning to her charkha. "Let me try this again. I got this charkha this morning. It just takes some practice," she said, fiddling with the wheel. "Every Indian should consider it his or her duty to learn how to use this." She turned the wheel with her right hand but suddenly winced. "Ouch!" A few drops of crimson emerged from her left hand. Without realizing it, Anjali sprang from her seat to her mother's side.

"Are *you* okay?"

Her mother nodded. "Just a little mishap with the spindle. It really is so hot in here. Do you want to try?"

Anjali stared at her struggling mother and softened. Her own knuckles were now pink, but the pain was fading. She took what was left of the raw cotton from her mother and turned the wobbly knob of the wheel, mimicking what Ma had done. The knob on the wheel was old and clumsy, hard to turn. It made a rickety noise until Anjali tilted her hand, then suddenly ran smoothly. In no time at all, all the raw cotton in Anjali's hand was gone, transformed into sleek strands of thread.

Anjali looked proudly at the thread. She had actually done it. She had made the beginnings of homespun clothes. Just like Gandhiji.

She turned to her mother and smiled. Maybe her mother's new job as a freedom fighter wouldn't be so awful.

CHAPTER 8

A month had passed since Anjali's mother had begun spinning. She had gotten quite good at it and said it was as calming as meditation. She would spin for an hour daily, and had outfitted the family in khadi both spun by her and bought at a store in the business district that only sold homespun goods. And she would go to the business district every morning after seeing Anjali off to school to teach others how to spin.

Anjali, enjoying her Sunday morning in the cow shed with Nandini, was dressed from head to toe in white khadi made by her mother. She wouldn't admit it out loud, but the homespun cotton was much cooler than her foreign-made ghagra-cholis, although it could have just been the milder October sun that made her feel this way. She tugged at her short sleeves. The rougher fabric took some getting used to, but the ghagra-choli actually looked nice. Simple but nice.

Anjali's mother had taken the spun cotton thread to a loom in the business district and returned with cloth. Jamuna had stitched the material into a short-sleeved choli and ankle-length ghagra, and Anjali was already in the process of unintentionally getting it dirty as she swung from one of the railings that held the shed's roof.

Anjali's father had told her hanging would help her grow tall so she could be as big and strong as the British. She couldn't tell if he was teasing her or being serious but thought it was better to be on the safe side and do it every day, just in case.

She held the wooden beam firmly with both her hands, ignoring the slight tugs of pain in her armpits and the coarse feeling of the khadi cloth on her legs. Anjali closed her eyes, inhaling deeply. It was almost peaceful, almost serene, almost—

"Anjali!"

Anjali shrieked, losing her grip, and fell to the ground, just missing the trough of water. She groaned, rubbing her bottom and wishing that she had bothered to put more straw down on the soil. She glared at the perpetrator. "Irfaan . . ."

He smelled faintly like copper, the way boys always smelled to Anjali when they had been running under the hot sun, and had an armful of bananas.

"Sorry."

"What are you doing with all those bananas, greedy goat?"

"I'm late for prayers, but I wanted to give Nandini some. It's Ammi's birthday."

Anjali gave Irfaan a tiny smile as he gently fed bunches of tiny, unpeeled yellow bananas to the cow. Irfaan's mother had died years ago from smallpox, the same disease that had killed Chachaji's wife and son.

"Happy birthday to Auntie," Anjali said softly as she gave Irfaan a sudden hug.

The sounds of the muezzin's loud voice echoed as he announced the Adhan, the Muslim call to prayer, from the nearby mosque. "I have to run." Irfaan raced out of the shed and propped himself up over the five-foot-tall back concrete wall to the back alley to get to his mosque on time.

Nandini finished gobbling up the bananas' skin

and fruit in a slobbery mess. Anjali dragged the metal trough of water out of her way, closer to Nandini. The cow gratefully dipped her head in and slurped the water. As the Adhan grew louder, Anjali gave Nandini a peck on the cheek and headed inside.

In the kitchen, Anjali's mother sat before their two-foot-tall carved wooden temple, dressed in her white khadi sari, palms together as she chanted her morning prayers. The room smelled strongly of the sandalwood incense sticks that were always lit during the puja. A bowl of dates sat before the temple as today's prasad, the offering placed before God during prayers and later eaten as a blessing. Anjali took a deep breath and quietly sat by her mother's side, watching as Ma lit a small lamp in front of the petite metal idols of gods. There was their family's idol, the goddess Annapurna, provider of food and nourishment, and a crawling baby Krishna. Behind them was a small idol of a cow, Kaamdhenu. To their side was a framed painting of the elephant-headed god Ganesh, sitting with his parents, Parvati and Shiva. Anjali loved watching Ma's peaceful face during her prayers reflected over the gods on the frame's glass pane.

Ma motioned to a small silver cup of water before

her. Anjali, following her mother's cue, poured the cup's contents over baby Krishna, bathing him. She put vermilion on the god's forehead and some on her own. Anjali closed her eyes tightly and was praying that God would take care of her family, Nandini, and Irfaan, when Chachaji's screams interrupted her.

"This is the height of disrespect!"

Anjali's eyes snapped open. She turned to Ma, who nodded for Anjali to go while singing her last prayer. Anjali rushed toward the livid shouts.

In the backyard, near the outhouse, Anjali saw Chachaji yelling at Mohan. The scrawny teenager was holding a broom made of long, dried stems that had been bundled together at the top in a makeshift handle and a large metal container for collecting excrement that he would carry away on his head.

"And where were you two days ago? What are we paying you for?"

"What's wrong?" asked Anjali.

"This boy is supposed to clean our toilets, and he hasn't shown up in four days."

Anjali hung back as Chachaji waved his wrinkled hand dramatically. Chachaji's bungalow in the big city of Bombay was not like theirs. It was modern. It had a water tank. Its latrine flushed into the sewer. It didn't need anyone to remove its waste, and he found the whole idea of a dry latrine sickening.

"God knows we can't be stuck with this filthy job fit only for Untouchables like you!" barked Chachaji, baring the few tartar-covered teeth he had left.

The boy looked down. "I was sick. I'm sorry."

"What should I do? Take your broom and clean it myself?" The wrinkles in Chachaji's face intensified. "If I touch your broom I'll get sick. I'll get smallpox and die."

"Chachaji. That's enough," came the stern voice of Anjali's mother. "Mohan, here, have some prasad."

"Sh-Shailaja . . ." stammered Chachaji, using Ma's first name. "This is unheard of."

Anjali's mother ignored Chachaji and tried to hand the boy a date. Mohan shook his head and backed away in fear, glancing at Chachaji.

Anjali's mouth suddenly went as dry as the desert. What was Ma doing? Untouchables weren't allowed to enter temples in their town, for fear that they would pollute them with their presence. How could Mohan eat the prasad? People would hurt him if they heard.

"It's bad enough that you let Anjali treat that Muslim

boy like her brother. And now *this*?" thundered Chachaji. Chachaji had never liked Irfaan. It made Anjali's stomach churn to hear the poisonous words of hate that Chachaji sometimes spewed, but now, as she stared at what Ma was trying to do, Anjali found her mouth hanging open. But she couldn't say anything to stop Chachaji . . . or Ma.

"Don't be scared, Mohan. Have some," Anjali's mother continued, but it was no use.

Mohan swooped the metal container onto his head and raced off the property, dropping his broom in his hurry.

"That's right. Run. Now who is going to pick up your filthy broom?" yelled Chachaji as he fumed into the house, slamming the door in a tantrum fit for a child.

Anjali's mother cinched her sari, tucking more fabric into her waistband, and went over to the broom and picked it up. Without a word, she headed for the outhouse with it.

Anjali's stomach grew queasy. "What are you doing? He's an Untouchable! You're not supposed to touch what he has touched, or you'll be unclean!"

Anjali's mother responded by opening the rusty green door to the outhouse, allowing the foulest of odors to escape. Anjali tried not to gag as her mother used Mohan's broom to sweep away at the dirt on the floor, guiding it toward the floor drain with the metal bucket of water from the outhouse corner.

Anjali just watched in silence. There were people to do this kind of work. As much as she despised the way Chachaji treated Mohan, there was some truth to what he'd said. Untouchables always cleaned the bathrooms. That was just how it was.

"Are you going to get sick now?" Anjali's lips trembled with the worry that her mother would get smallpox just like Irfaan's mother.

"Don't be silly, Anju. We never taught you such things. We have always told you that people are people, regardless of their religion or caste."

"Yes, but at school the other kids say—"

"The other kids don't know what they're talking about. Do not let others scare you out of doing what is right. Gandhiji has been trying to eliminate the idea of calling people Untouchables for years," Anjali's mother replied, sweeping slimy sludge formations from behind the toilet. "See, our leaders divided people into castes thousands of years ago to ensure that everyone did the work that was needed for the society to function. The unfortunate Untouchables got stuck with the dirty work. Over the years, the Untouchables got a terrible stigma attached to them for no fault of their own. That's why Gandhiji refers to them as Harijans, as a reminder to us, that they too are children of God. No better or worse than us." She wiped a hand on her side, smudging her hips brown.

Anjali cringed as her mother hunched behind the toilet, cleaning away the filth. "You're getting so dirty. You're going to look like them."

"We should be thanking them for cleaning up this mess. Why are *they* dirty for cleaning it? It's *our* mess, isn't it?" Anjali's mother sighed, sweat dripping down the parting in her hair and smearing her bindi. "When do we say you shouldn't cut your nails?"

Anjali didn't understand what this had to do with Untouchables. "At night."

"And you aren't supposed to wash your hair on Mondays, or your brother will get sick. So you don't wash your hair on Mondays for Irfaan, because he is like your brother, right?"

Anjali nodded.

"Those are superstitions, Anjali. They're not facts. They're just tales passed down generation to generation for a societal purpose. You probably aren't supposed to cut your nails at night because you could get hurt cutting in the dark, or someone could step on the clippings in the dark and get hurt that way too. Not washing your hair one day a week? That is probably meant to conserve water, because girls have long hair that needs a lot of water to wash. This irrational fear of people, calling them Untouchable, that is probably all there just to keep the status quo. To keep things as they are. To not challenge the system. But it's wrong, Anjali. It's just plain wrong."

"If it's so wrong, why has an Untouchable always cleaned our toilet?" asked Anjali.

Her mother shook her head. "Because your father and I didn't think to challenge the status quo. We were wrong too. But we won't make that mistake again. If all Indians can't even be equal in one another's eyes, how can we blame the British for considering themselves better than us?"

Anjali's mother wiped her brow. "Come with me tonight. You'll never think this way again."

But as she watched her mother's pure white home-spun sari get stained from the filth, all Anjali could think of was the waste of weeks of their hard work.

CHAPTER 9

*I*t was almost time for the meeting. Anjali's mother had washed up and changed into a simple pale lotus-pink sari. It wasn't made by Anjali or her mother, but it had been made in India and dyed with berry juice.

Anjali stood in the kitchen as Ma served her father a plate with steaming rice, lentils, chapati—a puffed-up flatbread, with hot air still trapped inside its layers of wheat—and bitter gourd in spicy gravy.

Baba smiled at Ma. "If I were to make a list of the bravest people I know, it would be you and my mother."

Ma's cheeks burned as pink as her sari at the compliment. She put her hand gently on Anjali's shoulder and steered her to the main hall, where Chachaji was involved in a game of solitaire with yellowed paper cards. He didn't bother to look their way.

"Chachaji, Jamuna will serve your dinner whenever you're hungry. We'll be back in a few hours."

"You could eat with Baba now while the food is hot," added Anjali, hoping her grumpy great-uncle would respond.

Chachaji put down his last card and sighed, finally looking at Anjali and her mother. "When I was a young boy, there was a man down the road from us who raised cows for milk."

Anjali glanced at her mother. This was the most Chachaji had said since the Mohan incident.

The old man continued. "He wasn't well off. He just lived on the milk he could sell. He could afford to keep the female cows that were born so their mothers could make milk and one day they could make milk too, but had no use for any male calves. And no farmer nearby needed to buy one off him. They had their own. So every time a male calf was born, he would kill it to save himself the cost of raising it for nothing."

Anjali's stomach fluttered, thinking of Nandini's pregnancy and how awful that man was for murdering an innocent calf.

"Chachaji . . . ," Anjali's mother said, putting a comforting hand on Anjali's back.

"She should hear this," he answered. "You both should. I loved cows as much as Anjali does. I hated what that man was doing. So you know what I did? The next time a male calf was born on that farm, I stole it."

Anjali couldn't believe what she was hearing. Her great-uncle had actually stood up for something?

"I ran away with that calf. I fed it milk from a little cup. I carried it around with me all day, despite how heavy it was and how skinny I was. And then you know what happened?"

Anjali shook her head, trying not to laugh at the thought of grumpy Chachaji saving a cow.

"The farmer found me."

Anjali's smile faded.

"He snatched the calf out of my arms and killed it right there in front of me."

Anjali backed away, brushing Ma's hand off her back. "Why are you telling me this?"

"I'm telling you this," the old man answered, "I'm telling you both this because that is what happens when you try to stand up for something. When you try to change things. It doesn't work. And worse, someone can get hurt. Or die."

Ma shook her head. "We're late," she said, ushering Anjali out the door. "Ignore him, Anju," she whispered as they headed down the dusty slate stairs to the even dustier driveway. She bolted the iron gate behind them and hailed a rickshaw.

A scrawny, shirtless man whose ribs could be seen through his skin pulled his bicycle rickshaw to a stop. His once off-white clothes were now the color of soot, and he wore scraps of cloth wrapped around his head in a makeshift turban.

"To the business district," said Anjali's mother as the two of them climbed into the buggy attached to the bicycle. "The Khadi Shop. And please hurry. We're late."

The rickshawalla stood on his bike and, using all his strength, shoved down on the pedals with his bony but muscular legs, joining the traffic for the one-and-a-half-mile-long journey down the main road.

Is Chachaji right? Anjali wondered. *Is Ma's work as a freedom fighter dangerous? Is just going to this meeting dangerous? What if the police show up to arrest everyone?*

Anjali sat back in the buggy, taking in the sights as

the rickshaw made its way through the neighborhoods of their town, trying to forget what Chachaji had just told her. Trying to forget all the fears it brought to her mind.

First up was a line of marble artists, busy constructing enormous idols of deities. With Diwali just a few days away, they would be getting lots of business soon. The rickshaw passed Irfaan's dad, Farhan Uncle, burning some trash outside his dairy, then passed the cluster of earthen shacks at the Untouchables' basti. A few seconds later, the rickshaw neared Captain Brent's office.

Anjali stuck her head out the buggy and shouted, "Quit India!"

"Anjali," scolded her mother as she peeked out for a look. Suddenly she too screamed, "Jai Hind!"

"Ma!" Anjali giggled as her mother winked at her.

The rickshawalla's eyes widened. He pedaled as fast as he could to get them away from Captain Brent's street.

Anjali watched as the drape of her mother's sari flapped in the breeze. She smiled at the street dogs, at the dozens of bookstores and tea stalls, at the elaborately carved marble temple with orange triangular flags and brass bells hanging from the ceiling. She smiled at the occasional camel cart that passed them, at the peacocks walking slowly by the roadside, at the black buffalo bathing in a shallow pond, their tails flicking at flies, and at the man selling flavored ice candy on the side of the street.

For the first time, Anjali also noticed how many children stood in the streets, homeless and hungry, and her smile disappeared. The kids were sweeping the roads, carrying garbage, sitting on corners, holding their naked infant siblings, begging for money . . . it scared Anjali to think of herself in their position, trying to earn a living on the street. Could she do the jobs they had to? Would she be able to do what it would take to survive? She reached for her mother's dry but reassuring hands, squeezing the cracked palm. She could have been born into any of these households. She was glad her soul had been assigned to someone in Madhuban Colony, or she could have been homeless like these street children.

Anjali couldn't look at the kids anymore. *What's worse*, she wondered, *having to live on the footpath with no home, or living in the Untouchables' basti but being forced to clean other people's waste?*

"Do you think Mohan has ever gone to school?" she asked, thinking about their toilet cleaner.

"Most of society wouldn't allow that in our town."

"If the Untouchables—sorry, the Harijans—if they're just like us, shouldn't they be allowed to go to school with us?"

Ma just stared outside blankly, like her eyes weren't taking any of the sights in, lost in thought as the rickshaw turned hastily through the crowded streets of the business district.

The more Anjali thought about it, the more unfair it seemed. Mohan was a few years older than her, but he had never been to school. While she was reading poems and learning arithmetic, Mohan was cleaning other people's sewage, not because he wanted to but because he was forced to by caste and circumstance. And he would be stuck doing this job he never chose his entire life. His entire unfair, miserable life.

Anjali squealed as the rickshaw turned on its rickety wheels, nearly hitting the concrete walls along the narrow lane they turned onto. The tiny passageway was much more cramped than the wide roads where Anjali lived. There barely was room for one rickshaw to fit in some parts of the alleys, filled with pedestrians and makeshift vendor stalls, and sometimes two would try to squeeze in, side by side.

At last, the rickshaw narrowly missed a stray cow on the street and came to a sudden halt in front of a four-story building with numerous cracked coats of light blue paint on the edge of the business district. There was nothing more past this store than a lone road leading to the crematorium grounds on the riverbank. Anjali and her mother hopped out of the rickshaw, and Ma handed the rickshawalla the bronze, diamond-shaped coins for their fare.

"Shall we?" Ma's face beamed with excitement.

Anjali followed her into the Khadi Shop. They passed stacks and stacks of homespun ghagra-cholis and saris. Many were white, but some were dyed colors too, mango-orange shawls and indigo-blue skirts. Anjali eyed the clothes with desire.

"Come, Anju, we're late," Ma called as she hurried up a wobbly spiral wooden staircase.

Anjali scurried up the stairs, holding tightly to the railing as each wobbly step shook a little with her weight. They passed another floor of clothes for women, men, and children. The third floor had dozens of spinning wheels. Flat ones, like the one her mother used, and tall standing ones, with a large upright wheel. Behind them were looms to weave the thread into fabric. Anjali glanced up. Ma was already entering the next floor, so Anjali hurried up the narrow stairs to join her in the fourth-floor attic.

The small room was packed with fifty freedom fighters, men and women, Hindu and Muslim, dressed from head to toe in khadi.

"This is where I've been teaching spinning," whispered Ma as she and Anjali squeezed into the crowd.

A mustached man with a U-shaped scar on his forehead stood in the front of the room, continuing his speech in a vaguely familiar, scholarly accent: "We have had many incidents with Captain Brent this past week. I know in many cases, normal people would have reacted to his impertinent behavior with violence. I commend all of you for reacting with nonviolence, with ahimsa."

The man adjusted his boat-shaped hat which the male freedom fighters all wore. "There have been rumors that Captain Brent will be attempting to shut down this very store and the spinning we do up here. I very much doubt he will do such a drastic thing, and even if he does, we must remain calm and not retaliate with violent means. An eye for an eye will leave the whole world blind."

It suddenly dawned on Anjali: he was the man from the radio.

"With Gandhiji and so many of our leaders imprisoned unjustly, we now, more than ever, must keep the light in this world, friends," said the mustached man, his voice sounding much clearer in person than on the static-filled radio. "Although Captain Brent has already stopped many of our shoppers from entering this very store, we must not let him stop us. We must continue making homespun on our own."

"Hear, hear, Keshavji!" said the freedom fighters.

"And we must continue our work in the bastis we have pledged to help in our neighborhoods."

Ma stood up, introducing herself to the crowd. "I'm Shailaja Joshi from Madhuban Colony. And my daughter brought it to my attention that the Harijan children in our neighborhood deserve an education too. So next week, as soon as the Diwali holidays are over, she and I are going to go to their basti after school to educate the children."

Although the thought of interacting with the Harijan kids made Anjali a little nervous, she couldn't help but smile proudly at her mother as the other free-dom fighters applauded. Chachaji was wrong. You had to stand up for what you believed in. You had to try to make a change, even if it was dangerous.

Keshavji nodded. "It's a wonderful idea, sister. And you too, beta," he said to Anjali. "I'll be happy to help you get started. I'll meet you there after the holidays." Keshavji turned to the crowd. "Every little bit we do makes a difference. This is a fight for independence on two fronts, inside and out. We must continue to protest the British and their unfair rules. And we must improve our society from within. What good is a free India when its people do not consider their brothers and sisters their equals? Social reform and civil disobedience must go hand in hand. For when all Indians are finally equal, no one can stop us. Freedom will one day be ours. It will be the sweetest nectar we drink, and we will drink it together, my friends. This I promise."

The crowd roared. Anjali's mother clapped her hands high above her head.

"Jai Hind. Till we meet again," concluded Keshavji, as he descended from the tiny stage at the front of the room.

Anjali stood up with her mother as they were almost forced down the stairs by the crowd's momentum.

"Who is Keshavji, Ma?" asked Anjali, trying to step down as carefully as she could with the crowd pushing behind her. "He is such a good speaker."

"Keshavji Parmar." Anjali's mother smiled. "He studied law in London. He stayed in Gandhiji's ashram, helped the Indian National Congress come up with legislation . . ." her mother continued as they landed on the ground floor of the store.

Anjali headed past the piles of exquisite clothes for the door.

"And oh, yes," added Ma. "Did I mention he is a Harijan?"

Anjali came to a sudden stop at the exit, staring at her mother in shock as throngs of freedom fighters of unknown religion and caste made their way past her in a sea of white khadi.

CHAPTER 10

A burst of iridescent red-and-white lights lit up the November night sky with a roar. Even though the fireworks had been going off every night this week for Diwali, every time it happened, startled pigeons and parrots would flutter away in terror, and Ma's hand would slip as she strung a thin needle with white thread through the tiny star-shaped jasmine blooms in her hand.

"Careful, Ma," said Anjali, swinging her legs impatiently from the edge of her bed as she waited for her jasmine garland to be finished. She didn't wear them often, but Ma always took the time to make two loops of jasmine for each of Anjali's braids for every holiday.

Diwali was one of Anjali's favorite holidays. The

whole town would be lit up with oil lamps for the festival of lights. Diwali meant a lot of things to a lot of different Hindus. For some, the lamps were lit to welcome the goddess of wealth to their home, helping her find her way on a dark night. For others, it signified the triumphant return from exile of the righteous god Ram. And for still others, it signified the end of the year and the start of a new one. But for Anjali, Diwali was just a beautiful, joyous time to get a break from school and spend time with her family, eating, laughing, singing, playing cards, and exchanging gifts.

"Where does Keshavji live?" Anjali asked as Ma finished threading the jasmine.

"His home is in the business district," Ma answered, tying the ends of her jasmine string together into a loop, and pinning it to the right side of Anjali's hair.

Anjali took a deep breath, inhaling the sweet perfume. "In another Harijan basti?"

Anjali's mother paused in the middle of making another loop. "Do you live in the Brahmin basti by the river?"

Anjali shook her head.

"Hold still," Anjali's mother said, pinning the second

loop to Anjali's left braid. "Not every Harijan lives in a basti. Just as not every Brahmin lives in a bungalow. Keshavji's house is near the shop where our meeting was held."

Anjali turned to face the mirrors on the double doors of her wooden armoire.

One side was used for making sure you were painting your bindi on in place, centered between your eyebrows like a third eye. The other door's mirror had been painted over with the image of a river winding through grassy hills. Anjali loved staring at the painting on that door, especially the right corner, where peacocks frolicked along the lush green riverbank. Whenever she brought home a bad report from school, she would stare at that river and imagine skipping with the colorful birds.

She turned her attention from the birds to her own reflection and beamed. The garlands looked perfect, and their deep floral scent made Anjali feel as beautiful as those fancy British women she had seen in Captain Brent's last summer.

I bet if they saw me now they wouldn't be laughing at me, Anjali thought.

People always wore their best clothes for Diwali. And

though this was the time of year Anjali looked forward to most, excited to get a set of new, richly colored ghagras, she had gotten used to the feel of the khadi clothes she had been wearing for months. Her parents had given her a teal ghagra from the Khadi Shop for today, the last day of Diwali. It had a magenta-and-parrot-green border on the skirt and parrot-green polka dots on the blouse. It wasn't as fancy as the clothes she wore on Diwalis past, but Anjali still loved it. And she felt proud to wear something made in her own land, by Indian hands.

"Think Keshavji will be upset you're going without him?" she asked.

"Why would he?" Ma retorted, taking a quick glance in the mirror to straighten her sari. "What we are doing is a nice gesture. It will make everything go even smoother after Diwali when Keshavji helps us."

Jamuna entered the room in a new purple khadi sari Anjali's parents had given her for Diwali. "Your sweets have cooled," she said to Anjali's mother.

Ma nodded, sweeping a cotton shawl with embroidered flowers on it over her shoulders. She had spent the morning making a large batch of savory namkeen, fried flour with carom seeds. And she had worked all afternoon making trays of sweets of different flavors, roasting chickpea flour in ghee for the besan ladoo, shredding coconut for coconut barfi, and grinding almonds and cardamom into a paste for the badam barfi. Their little table was overflowing with delicacies. She had set two of the trays in front of their little home temple as an offering to the gods, and now, with the prayers done and the treats and prasad finally cooled, everyone could finally taste them.

Anjali and her mother headed to the kitchen. "Give the prasad to your father and Chachaji, and then we can be on our way," said Ma.

Anjali nodded. "Don't forget about Irfaan. He's coming too."

Anjali's mother smiled. "How could I forget?"

There in the kitchen, hunched over the table full of sweets, was Irfaan, gobbling up the badam barfi.

"Greedy goat." Anjali giggled.

Irfaan blushed sheepishly, his mouth stuffed, as he handed Anjali a small tin of crayons.

The last day of the Diwali celebrations was Anjali's favorite. It was a day celebrating the bond between brothers and sisters. Sisters would give their brothers sweets, and in return, their brothers would give them presents and promise to take care of their sisters. Irfaan always gave Anjali crayons, and Anjali always gave Irfaan a bundle of the badam barfi, since it was his favorite. And at Eid-al-Fitr, they would trade, with Irfaan giving Anjali sweets and Anjali giving Irfaan crayons.

"Thank you!" Anjali exclaimed as she eagerly eyed the bright colors of the new beeswax crayons. She inhaled their earthy aroma and felt their sharpened points. She couldn't wait to draw with them.

Ma handed Anjali one of the two prasad trays as they headed into the hall. Anjali gave a ladoo to her father and bowed to him in pranaam. He raised his hand over her head to bless her. She then put a ladoo in front of Chachaji, who was busy reading his newspaper.

Chachaji shook his head.

"What's wrong?" Anjali asked.

"I don't want to eat anything that's going . . . to *them*."

Anjali's heart thumped in her chest. "Why? Do you think they are polluting it from a distance before they even see the food?"

"Anjali," her father said gently, "it's Diwali. Now is not a time for arguments."

"Fine." Anjali picked the tray up and turned her back

on Chachaji. "Don't eat it. More for them." Deliberately skipping her bow to Chachaji, she headed out with her tray, Ma and Irfaan behind her. If that old man was going to be so hateful, he didn't deserve her respect.

As they headed out the gate, past dozens of clay lamps with wicks dancing above hot ghee, Ma tucked a strand of hair behind Anjali's ear. "Anju, you have to be more patient. Some people need more time."

Anjali stopped in her tracks. Suman and Lakshmi Auntie were right there in front of their house, pouring handfuls of colored powder into intricate designs outside their gate. Lakshmi Auntie's giant bindi seemed even bigger than usual for the holidays. And Suman was dressed in the most gorgeous ghagra-choli Anjali had ever seen. It was a deep magenta with gemstones on the blouse and intricate bright green parrots embroidered all over the skirt. Anjali's fingers ran over the simple green dots on her own blouse and couldn't help but feel bad, even if it was just for a minute.

"Who are the lucky people? Getting so many sweets?" Lakshmi Auntie smiled.

"The Harijans," answered Ma.

Lakshmi Auntie's face dropped as she gave Ma the coldest of stares.

"And some people will never change no matter how much time you give them," said Anjali, as the trio headed for Mohan's basti.

CHAPTER 11

*A*s Anjali and Irfaan followed Ma to the basti, Anjali felt a little nervous.

"Are you going to talk to them?" Irfaan whispered to her.

"Of course I'm not going to talk to them. What would I say to them? 'Sorry we have been so mean to you for so long'?" Anjali hissed back, ignoring the putrid odors of rotting garbage and human waste dancing around her nose.

Just outside the basti, alongside the main road, a woman and her naked baby were sitting on the ground. Ma stopped suddenly, her lips trembling as she searched for words. She whisked the cotton shawl off her shoulders and gave it to the woman. "Please. He must be so cold."

The woman put her palms together in a grateful namaste and draped the shawl over her child, but Ma just kept staring at them.

"What is it, Ma?" asked Anjali. "Do you not want to go in?"

Anjali's mother shook her head. "No. Of course I want to go in. Come." She headed toward the small clearing in front of the shacks. Anjali nodded at Irfaan to go first. He nervously shook his head. Anjali sighed and led the way into the grungy grounds.

A crowd of a dozen women and children were sitting in a circle in front of their tiny earthen homes, a little two-foot-by-one-foot herb garden to their side. Mohan sat with them, clapping and singing songs as a wrinkly old woman and the little girl who saw Anjali paint the Q danced inside the circle, celebrating Diwali. But as soon as they saw the outsiders, they came to a standstill.

Anjali's mother cleared her throat. "Happy Diwali!" She smiled a little too widely.

Anjali's stomach dropped. If her mother apprehensive, Anjali was terrified. Maybe she and Ma shouldn't pass out prasad. Maybe it was a bad idea. Mohan had come to remove the waste from their toilet every other morning since that day last month, out of fear of Chachaji. Change could be scary, and it seemed like today's change was shocking to everyone as they stood there in silence, staring at one another.

Ignoring a mosquito buzzing by her ear, Anjali took a deep breath, entered the broken circle of stunned people, and approached the little girl and the old lady. The girl was tightly clinching her necklace of round brown seeds. "I'm Anjali. What's your name?"

The girl squeezed the old lady's hand.

"It's okay."

"Paro." The girl hesitated. "My name is Paro."

"I like your necklace, Paro."

"Mohan made it."

Anjali smiled. Silently reminding herself that Paro would not make her sick or dirty, she took a badam barfi from her tray and offered it to Paro.

"It's prasad," said Anjali's mother, her voice less shaky.

A gasp went through the crowd.

"What are you trying to do? You'll get us killed!" said the old woman, pulling Paro back.

Ma shook her head. "Aren't you sick of being treated as if you were less than human? If you want things to change, you have to change them. As Gandhiji says, if we change ourselves, the tendencies in the world will also change."

"The world will change?" The woman held up her wrinkly left arm. There were blistery red scars all over it. "As a child in my village, I was sick of having to walk four times as far as others to the well the Untouchables were allowed to use and decided to just draw water from the well down the lane. The well the higher-caste people used. You know what the villagers did to me? They held my arm over lit coals to teach me a lesson, then filled the well with rocks, saying no one could drink from it now that I had polluted it. I was forced to leave my village, my home," she added, choking back tears. "My arm has never been right since. Maybe people like you Brahmins can do what you want and make great changes. But not us."

Ma spoke, tears in her eyes. "We have to try. Together we can change things. First, stop calling yourself an Untouchable. You're not." She bent down and gave Paro a hug. "See? Nothing has happened to me. You're a Harijan. A child of God. And you deserve to be able to eat the blessings from God too."

From his spot in what was once a celebratory circle, Mohan scoffed, shaking his head at the whole scene.

A small breeze blew through the basti as Ma took the old woman's hand in hers. "I'm sorry for what was done to you. If things were to change, no one else would have to suffer like you did." Ma offered her the prasad.

The woman stared at her scars, blinking back tears.

The clothes on the clothesline between the shacks shivered in the wind as Anjali's mother's voice wavered. "Please . . . teach these children that things should change. That this time they actually can change. Please?"

The woman glanced at Paro and slowly nodded. "My granddaughter should never go through what I did." And with that, the old lady took two pieces of prasad from Ma's tray, gave one to Paro, and took a bite.

Paro eagerly chewed the sweet almond treat.

Anjali slowly went up to Mohan. "Badam barfi?" she asked. But Mohan just turned away and stormed into the maze of huts behind them.

Before Anjali's own tears but could spill, another boy stepped forward. "Is it real badam?" he asked.

Anjali nodded.

"I've never had badam before."

"It's my best friend's favorite," Anjali said as Irfaan gave her an encouraging smile. "Want to try it?"

The boy ate it in one bite. He grinned. "I think this is my favorite too."

Slowly, more and more children, men, and women approached, taking the prasad. All Anjali's nervousness faded away. This was working. Things were starting to change.

Anjali noticed Paro was now squatting by the methi plant in the little garden, staring at a torn piece of newspaper. "I saw you with a newspaper a few months ago too. Do you like the pictures in them?" she asked the little girl as Irfaan joined them.

"I collect them for Mohan," Paro replied. She turned the paper so Anjali and Irfaan could see the black-and-white images on the front.

Leela Chitnis beamed back at Anjali in a still from her latest movie, dressed in a beautiful sari and a necklace of seashells. At the bottom of the page was an advertisement for a jeweler with a necklace of round beads.

"That almost looks like the necklace you're wearing," said Irfaan.

"He can make almost any necklace out of the seeds and shells and wood he finds."

"That's amazing," said Anjali.

"Is it true your neighbor looks like Leela Chitnis?" Paro asked.

Anjali stopped smiling. "What?"

"Your neighbor. Mohan says she is as beautiful as Leela Chitnis."

Anjali sighed. She couldn't deny Suman's beauty, and her gorgeous ghagra-cholis just made her seem even more like a movie star. "Yes, she does look like Leela Chitnis." Anjali glanced at the last sweet left on her tray. "Where does Mohan live?"

Paro pointed to a dingy house to the side.

Irfaan nodded to Anjali. "I'll wait for you."

Anjali headed toward the home with the tray. She stopped at the entrance and peered in. Mohan was sitting on the floor next to a small, flickering clay lamp. His back to Anjali, he was stringing tiny wooden beads into a necklace, occasionally glancing at an image of a necklace in the torn newspaper on the dirt floor beside him. He'd obviously carved the beads himself with the tools next to him, and each bead had a hand-drilled hole that allowed him to create his necklaces.

"You're really talented," Anjali said softly from the doorway.

Mohan turned, clearly startled.

"The fair is in a couple months, in January," said Anjali, thinking about her favorite visiting fair. The artisans from the villages west of Navrangpur were known for their intricate embroidery, stitching mirrors into shawls, ghagras, purses, little toy cloth horses, elephants, camels, and the clothing of wooden puppets. People came from all across town to attend the fair, see the amazing talent there, and of course, buy the goods.

"You should sell your necklaces there," Anjali continued, nearing Mohan. "You could just walk through the fair and sell them. No one would stop you. And I'm sure lots of my neighbors would love them. They wouldn't care who made them." Anjali was only half-lying. After all, if the girls in her class never knew who made the necklaces, they would love them.

"Not even when they saw me?" Mohan mumbled, continuing to string the beads.

"What?" asked Anjali, not sure she had heard him correctly.

Fear flashed in Mohan's eyes. "Sorry," he said, looking back down again.

Anjali shook her head. "You don't have to apologize. Just tell me what you were saying."

Mohan paused. "If your neighbors saw me at the fair, they'd recognize me as their toilet cleaner, wouldn't they? If they are too scared to even touch my fingers when they pay me for cleaning their waste, what makes you think they'd buy a necklace I made with those fingers, let alone wear it?"

"We'll tell them you're a Harijan, not an Untouchable," Anjali said, hoping this would help. "Just like Gandhiji said."

But Mohan just scoffed again. "Your Gandhi is wrong. Calling us children of God is talking down to us. It's insulting. And it solves nothing. It's just a word!" His voice rose. "Everyone will still think of us as dirty and beneath them. Changing what you call someone doesn't fix the problems behind the name." He dropped the necklace he'd been working on, scattering beads across the ground.

Anjali felt terrible for upsetting Mohan and wanted

to help him clean up, but she knew it would be best to just leave him alone. "I'll . . . just leave your prasad here," she said, crouching down to put the last barfi on the newspaper near Mohan. He didn't look up. "Happy Diwali," Anjali said softly as she headed for the exit.

She heard the faint crinkling of newspaper and turned. The prasad was no longer on the newspaper.

CHAPTER 12

Anjali couldn't stop thinking about what Mohan had said to her. Could Gandhiji actually be wrong about something? Did that make her mother's involvement in Gandhiji's movement wrong? She kept twisting and turning in bed that night, her legs getting tangled in her grandmother's old wool shawl she was sleeping under, her mind consumed with questions and thoughts. Was it really wrong to say "Harijan"? And if so, why didn't Gandhiji realize the name was hurtful? And if "Untouchable" was wrong and "Harijan" was wrong, what was right?

The next morning, as Ma massaged Anjali's hair with coconut oil, Anjali couldn't keep quiet any longer.

"Mohan doesn't want to be called 'Harijan,' Ma," she said softly. "He said it's insulting."

"Insulting?" Ma untangled Anjali's hair with her fingers. "Gandhiji picked such a beautiful word. How could it be insulting to be called a child of God? Isn't that a good thing?"

"He said it doesn't solve anything."

"Of course it does. It reminds anyone who thinks otherwise that they are also children of God, just like anybody else. After all, Gandhiji said so."

Could there really only be one right way? And if Ma refused to call Mohan what he wanted to be called, and kept calling him a name he found insulting, how could Anjali face him the next time she saw him? Anjali fought the urge to scratch at her scalp as the oil trickled this way and that, tickling her, drumming her fingers over and over again on her ghagra.

Anjali was so restless the rest of the day that her father took her down the street to their corner paanwalla to cheer her up. There was just one more day off work and school during this Diwali holiday, so Anjali tried to enjoy it.

She and Baba wished their neighbors a happy Diwali as they passed them. At the end of the road was a long line of customers, waiting for their turn at the corner stall where the paanwalla sold his treats.

Anjali smiled as an elderly couple approached the line. She didn't know their names but recognized them from the next street over. She passed their bungalow on her way to Irfaan's.

"Namaste," Baba greeted them with his hands together. "Please. Go ahead," he gestured, in front of Anjali in line.

The couple smiled gratefully and took their place in front of Anjali.

Veena Auntie, their widowed neighbor from the house at the end of the street, just next to the paanwalla's corner shop, exited her property with her son and his wife. She was dressed all in white.

Baba once again smiled and gestured for them to go in front of Anjali in line. Anjali smiled politely at Veena Auntie, who was now in front of her, and turned to whisper to her father. "Baba, if you keep this up, we will get paan next year."

"This reminds me of Akbar and Birbal," Baba said, fanning Anjali's face with the bottom of her braid.

Anjali tried not to smile. Her father had told her the same dozen stories of the Muslim emperor Akbar and his clever Hindu minister Birbal for as long as she could remember.

"Emperor Akbar once decided to build a new palace on a scenic spot that just happened to be where an old widow lived in a hut. She didn't want to leave her home. So Birbal began filling sacks with mud from around the hut to help clear the site for construction to begin. He tried to lift one bag—"

"But he couldn't." Anjali could recite this story by heart. "Akbar said, 'That bag is too heavy.' Birbal said, 'This is just one bag of mud. Imagine how heavy the widow's burden is, having to carry thousands of bags of memories out of her home that you want to destroy.'"

Baba nodded. "Exactly."

"But what does that have to do with my paan?" asked Anjali, whose stomach was beginning to rumble.

"Even without an emperor forcing her out of her home, a widow has plenty of burdens. She is forced to wear white—"

"Like a freedom fighter in khadi," said Anjali.

"Yes, but the difference is most widows don't have a choice. They aren't supposed to wear colors after their husband dies. Some are even sent away by their husband's family so they don't get his money."

"You always let old women take cuts in line. That doesn't help them with their real problems. You can't lift everyone's burdens for them."

Baba sighed. "Do you know why I don't disagree with Chachaji when he says things that are wrong? Or why I put up with the way he acts sometimes?"

Anjali shook her head.

"My father died when I was in my last year of school before college. We lived with my uncle and his family."

"And now he lives with us," said Anjali, twisting her braid around her finger.

"No. This was a different uncle. He was my father's oldest brother."

Anjali let go of her hair. She had never heard of her father having another uncle.

"When my mother became a widow, that uncle took our shares of the family business. His wife took my mother's gold jewelry. They treated her like she was a burden. They yelled at her all day. We had no choice but to leave. But my mother didn't have a job outside the house. We had no income. We were so poor, Anjali. So poor. We had just one outfit each. It's why I was so upset when Ma burned perfectly usable clothes instead of giving them away."

Anjali couldn't believe it. Her father had been poor?

"That's when my father's youngest brother, who had moved to Bombay to start a new business, took us in. We lived with him and his wife, and I was able to finish up my last year of school and go to a university. My mother lived with them until she died. He never treated her like a burden, the way my other uncle had. He treated her as a sister. So decades later, when Chachaji was in danger, when his store was burned in the riots in Bombay, how could I not welcome him into my house, just as he had welcomed my mother and me?"

Anjali nodded. It suddenly made sense. Why Baba always had a soft spot for women who were helpless. Why he put up with Chachaji's nonsense. Why he didn't bat an eye when Ma joined the freedom movement.

"That's why I'm so proud of you and Ma. You're brave and strong. You'll never suffer the way my mother suffered."

Anjali gave her father's hand a little squeeze. At that moment, Veena Auntie walked by with her paan. "Your turn, beta," she said, patting Anjali on the head.

Anjali leaned over the paanwalla's counter and pointed to all the fillings she wanted in her betel nut leaf. She watched in anticipation as the paanwalla dabbed some lime paste onto the bright green leaf, then smeared a dark jam of rose petals and sugar on one side, sprinkled some shredded coconut, added a few fennel seeds, and then neatly folded the leaf into a tightly wrapped triangle. He held it all in place by stabbing a black clove through the layers.

Anjali momentarily forgot her worries as she bit into the damp, rubbery exterior and got to the sweet and refreshing stuffing. "Thanks, Baba," she said, wiping a bit of the jam from the corner of her mouth.

"It's good, isn't it? I was half-expecting to run into your paan-loving Masterji here."

Anjali shuddered at the thought of running into her teacher and his red teeth here, when Baba suddenly smiled at a young couple passing by with their paan. "Soni? What are you doing all the way over here? This must be your husband!"

The woman nodded. "My husband's cousins live on this side of town, Professor."

Baba nudged Anjali. "Anjali, this is Soni Deshpande. She was one of my brightest students. Oh, but you are married now. Soni . . . Malkar, right?"

"Actually, Professor, it's now Manju Malkar," she replied as her husband smiled politely. "I should get going. But it was nice to meet you, Anjali," Soni said, heading away.

"Bye, Soni—Manju," Anjali's father said, stumbling on his words.

"What's wrong, Baba?" asked Anjali as a flush of red splotched Baba's cheeks.

"She invited me to her wedding. I shouldn't have gotten her name wrong."

"But why did she change her first name too?" Anjali asked as she and Baba headed back down the street to their house.

"She's Marathi. In their tradition, the bride has her first and last name changed by her husband."

Anjali shrugged. "I would feel like I wasn't me. How would you even remember to respond when someone called you by your new first name?"

Baba shook his head. "If that's what she wants to be called, then we should respect that."

"And what if she doesn't want to be called that? What if her husband's family is forcing her to take his new name?"

"That's always a possibility too," said Baba. "But why all the questions about names? Are you getting married?" He grinned.

Anjali smiled at the bad joke. "No. I just . . . Yesterday, Mohan said Gandhiji was wrong to use the word 'Hari-jan.' He said the name was putting them down, like we were so superior. And he said it wouldn't change the way they were treated anyway."

Baba's forehead scrunched up, the way it did when he was working on a difficult engineering problem to teach his class. "Well . . . if he said that, we should respect it."

Baba was right. Ma was wrong. Anjali swallowed the last bite of her paan. Despite how tasty the treat was, she couldn't soothe the uneasy ache growing in her belly.

CHAPTER 13

$\mathcal{C}$lutching a newly shed peacock feather, Anjali breathed in deeply as she entered Mohan's basti. It was the Monday after Diwali. But it wasn't just the first day of school after the holidays. It was the day Anjali was going to help the freedom fight by doing more than just making her own clothes. It was going to be Mohan's, Paro's, and the other kids' first day of school ever at their basti.

That entire day at Pragati, Anjali could barely concentrate on what Masterji was saying. She was fidgeting so much, even he seemed to realize she was anxious about something, and spared her knuckles the ruler. As soon as school got out, Anjali and Irfaan raced out the doors and headed straight to the basti.

Ma was already outside the basti with Keshavji, talking to Paro's grandmother, the old woman with the burned arm. A couple other freedom fighters stood near Keshavji, deep in conversation. Keshavji smiled warmly at Anjali and Irfaan. "Welcome, beta. And you must be Irfaan. Shailajaji was just telling me all about you. There are several children here that I think you'd get along great with."

Anjali nodded. "We met during Diwali."

"Is that so?" Keshavji looked at Ma, folds of confusion appearing on his forehead.

Ma's cheeks turned red. "I was so excited to get started. And I had made all this prasad. I just thought it would be a nice gesture."

"Ah," Keshavji said after a bit of a pause. "I'm sure it was. Come." He led Anjali, Irfaan, Ma, and the other men into the basti.

The children were once again in the midst of a game of gilli danda.

Keshavji smiled at them. "Now, I just met these youngsters, but I'm pretty good with names. There's Dinanath, Suraj, Urmila, Jyoti, Vijay, Rohit, Seema,

Kavita, and Paro, right?" Paro nodded as she hit the gilli on one end with the danda, forcing it off the ground, and then swung the danda, hitting the gilli.

Anjali was so engrossed watching the game that she didn't even notice the harsh smells of the basti. Instead, she focused as the gilli went airborne.

Suraj and Urmila rushed forward, giggling as they tried to catch it. Unfortunately for them, no one did, and Paro got to measure the distance the gilli flew with her danda.

It was three times the length of the danda. "Three! I got three points again!" The scrawny girl laughed.

"That's right, beta. And what's three plus three?" asked a familiar voice.

Anjali and Irfaan turned to see Masterji standing there, his oily hair slicked back.

Anjali's jaw dropped. What was her teacher doing here?

The little girl counted on her fingers. "Six," she replied, beaming.

"You got it!" exclaimed Masterji, smiling his red-tinted teeth, his punishment ruler visibly absent.

"Your Masterji has agreed to come here after school

to help teach the children," explained Keshavji.

Anjali tried not to show her shock as she exchanged a glance with Irfaan. Masterji—cruel, impatient Masterji—was secretly a freedom fighter? And despite all his strict rules at school, he didn't care about the caste system rules?

"It's very nice to see the two of you helping out," added Masterji in the kindest voice Anjali could ever remember him using with her in all the years she had known him. He set up a tiny chalkboard by the clothesline near one of the homes. "Come now. It's time for class."

Paro and the other kids cheered as they dropped the gilli and danda and rushed to their makeshift classroom.

Anjali elbowed Irfaan. She had never seen children so excited to learn. The kids sat down cross-legged on the ground, blowing up a cloud of dust as they settled into their spots. Women and men, some as old as Chachaji, came out of the shacks to watch.

"All of you are welcome to join," said Anjali's mother, ushering the adults forward. She smiled at a shy child who was clinging to his mother's legs. "When I was your age," she said to him, "my classes used to be outside too, under a peepal tree. Please join us."

Anjali watched as some of the women refused to come forward, choosing instead to watch from a distance while shyly covering their heads with the loose ends of their frayed saris. Keshavji spoke to a few of them, but they just shook their heads. Anjali turned away. It was hard to look at the fear in the women's faces, but she couldn't blame them for not wanting to learn. After all, their whole lives they had been told that Untouchables couldn't enter schools.

Keshavji approached Ma, shaking his head. "They say to let the children learn. So I will leave you to it, Shailajaji. We must be going. We have to drop off some charkhas to the villages outside town before we need to record the next radio address. I look forward to hearing how today went at our next meeting." Keshavji bid farewell to everyone. "Jai Hind," he added, leaving with the two men.

At that moment, Mohan entered the basti. He looked tired, probably having just finished his day's work cleaning out latrines.

Anjali followed him, ducking under some

cotheslines a stray kitten was pawing at. Mohan paused outside his home, near a clay vessel from which he poured water to wash his hands. He glanced at Anjali. "How old are you? Nine? Ten?"

"Ten," Anjali said, standing taller. "That's why Ma lets me help her. I'm old enough."

Mohan nodded. "When I was nine, we lived in a different basti. My mother made me join her in cleaning toilets. She said I was old enough."

Anjali suddenly felt awful.

"I was so repulsed by the job, I threw up. I ran home crying. When she found me, I was so angry. I told her I would never go with her again. I'd never clean a toilet. It was disgusting."

"What did she say?" Anjali asked.

"Nothing. Not at first." Mohan wiped his hands on his shirt, drying them. "Instead, she hit me. She hit me over and over and over again and told me this was our place. This was what we had to do in life, so I had better get used to it. This was just how it was and nothing could ever change that. Then she hugged me. She held me. She told me we couldn't change what we did in life or how people thought of us. But we could change what we called ourselves. She told me about Dr. Ambedkar. He was one of us. But he had gone to school. He didn't have to clean toilets. And he had named us Dalits.

"It means 'oppressed,'" Mohan said. "It means we are born into a life of constant struggle because of this unfair caste system. It means what really has happened to us. I'm not like the others in this basti, grateful to be called 'Harijan.' I ate that prasad because I was hungry, not because I needed anyone's blessings. See, we aren't Harijans. We aren't children of your god. Your god forsook us long ago. Your god is not our god. So you can keep your prasad and your blessings. We don't need them. We are Dalits."

Anjali wasn't sure what to say. How could she and Ma have been so insensitive and brought prasad to the Dalits? Were they supposed to be grateful to have been given prasad when most temples didn't allow them inside? How oblivious had she and Ma been? She felt foolish and ashamed.

"Dalits," Anjali said slowly. It sounded like such a sad word. But maybe that was a realer word for what Mohan and his people had been through. Maybe she lived in a dream world. Maybe it was time to see with clear eyes that real problems in the world took time to solve.

"I'll tell Ma," she said. "We won't call you that other word ever again. I promise."

Mohan scanned Anjali's face as if he weren't sure if she could be trusted or not.

"I'm going to go back out and help Masterji and Ma teach numbers. Did you want to come?"

"Why? So I can write down how many containers of waste I pick up each day?"

"No. So you can write down prices to sell your necklaces at the fair," Anjali replied.

But Mohan just smiled at Anjali like she was still a silly little girl and headed into his home.

Knowing better than to bother him there again, Anjali headed back through the cluster of tiny homes until she got to the courtyard at the front of the basti. Masterji was writing the numbers one through ten on the chalkboard in Hindi. He recited them out loud, pointing to each digit with his ruler, and then turned to the class. "Now it's your turn to write."

The students, using small chalkboards Ma had bought, awkwardly gripped their chalk and began copying the numbers. Anjali, Irfaan, and Anjali's mother made their way around the class, checking on the students' work. Irfaan helped Jyoti switch the numbers seven and six so they were in the correct order. Anjali's mother encouraged Vijay, a timid little boy, to try to write the numbers, finally getting him to write the number one on his little chalkboard.

Anjali made her way beside the tiny garden, being careful not to step on the thriving coriander and methi plants. *If Chachaji saw how healthy their plants were compared to ours, he'd faint.* Anjali smiled to herself as she bent down by Paro's side.

Paro held a tattered newspaper, staring intently at the page numbers as she tried to copy them.

Anjali attempted to correct Paro's Hindi number four, as it was looking more like an English eight, but when Paro tried to copy the corrected digit, she still couldn't get it right. Without a second thought, Anjali took Paro's little hand in hers and guided her chalk on the board until she got the number four down perfectly.

Anjali beamed with pride. Behind her, someone cleared his throat. Anjali turned. It was Mohan.

Dinanath, Urmila, and some of the other children

stopped writing, eager to hear what Mohan had to say as Ma went to hand him a chalkboard and chalk.

"I knew it!" Anjali exclaimed. "You do want to learn to write numbers."

Mohan took the items from Ma and shook his head. "No. I want to learn to write letters. I want to learn to write 'Dalit.'" He sat down in front of Anjali. "I want to learn to write 'Dalit' so no one ever calls me a Harijan again."

CHAPTER 14

That evening, Anjali and Ma had gobbled down a spicy meal of lentils, rice, piping hot chapati, and okra stuffed with chickpea flour prepared by Jamuna before heading to the Khadi Shop. There wasn't a meeting planned, but Ma wanted to talk to Keshavji.

They found him on the third floor, spinning cotton into yarn as a young freedom fighter named Balkishan worked on the wooden loom, weaving freshly spun cotton into fabric. Anjali watched as Balkishan sat on a stool in front of the rectangular loom. His feet were taking turns pushing two pedals on the floor. With one hand, he yanked at a loop of thick string tied to the top of the loom. With the other, he repeatedly pulled a horizontal bar toward him and then pushed it away from him. The loom made a clickety-clack sound every time he completed the series of actions. And every time she heard the noise, a new row of fabric was woven above his lap.

Keshavji looked up from his charkha and smiled at Anjali. "Are you enjoying seeing the fabric of our independence growing here, beta? With each row that is woven, we are getting closer and closer to our goals."

Anjali nodded as Ma sat by Keshavji.

"I've made a terrible mistake," Anjali's mother told him. "When I went to the basti without you and gave everyone prasad, I thought I was making a huge difference in their world. Anjali told me how wrong that was. I—I don't know why I didn't realize it before."

Keshavji stopped spinning. "Sometimes it's hard to see everything going on in the garden when your nest is perched at the top of the tree."

Ma's ears burned red around her diamond flower earrings. "You sound like my neighbors. When I first started working for Captain Brent, I overheard some of them saying how perfect a fit it was for an elitist like me."

Keshavji shook his head. "I didn't mean you were an

elitist, sister. I meant you know your own world very well. It's just hard to see through the leaves sometimes when you have never been on the ground before. It's not an insult."

"But 'Harijan' is," Anjali said, joining Ma next to Keshavji. "Gandhiji calls the Dalits that, so we did too. We didn't know how insulting it was until now. Why would you want the blessings when you can't even enter the temple?"

Keshavji nodded. "It's why I'm a Buddhist. Not a Hindu."

"But shouldn't Gandhiji know better?" Ma asked. "He fasted for the Dalits a few decades ago. So they wouldn't be considered a separate class from everyone else."

"He fasted to stop the British from supporting the new constitution that was proposed. The one that would give Dalits their own separate representation for seventy years. Dr. Ambedkar, the Dalit leader, did not agree with Gandhiji's stance. He was stopping the Dalits from having a constitutional safeguard to ensure their voice would be heard."

"If Gandhiji is so wrong, why are you part of the Quit India movement?" Anjali asked.

The loom suddenly went silent as Balkishan stared at Anjali.

"Anjali!" Ma said, the color draining from her cheeks. She glanced at Balkishan. "Please carry on," she added, before turning to Anjali. Her voice dropped to a whisper. "You can't talk like that."

"It's okay," Keshavji replied. "It was an innocent question. It deserves an answer." He put his hand on Anjali's shoulder. "Beta, when I was younger, I lived in Gandhiji's ashram. I have worked beside him. I like many of his ideas. But I also like many of Dr. Ambedkar's ideas. I'm not part of the Quit India movement for Gandhiji. I'm part of the movement for India. Because I believe in freedom and equality for all people."

Anjali's shoulders slumped. It just didn't make sense. "How could Gandhiji be so wrong about this issue but so right on others?"

Keshavji shrugged. "I think you can care deeply about someone and still do the wrong thing."

"I'm afraid we are all too familiar with that," said Ma.

"It's okay, sister. If we make a mistake, we should apologize. We should learn from it. And we should change our ways. Like the cloth on that loom, we must take this new knowledge and better ourselves, row by row by row."

Anjali stared at the loom as Balkishan once again pedaled away. The cloth looked different now as it grew. It was no longer a series of visible rows of thread. It was a cohesive piece of white fabric, strong, united.

Keshavji once again began turning the wheel on his charkha, transforming the raw puff of cotton into yarn. "Perhaps you're realizing now that it isn't we Dalits who are backward. Who need to be saved, who need to change. But rather it is the rest of India."

CHAPTER 15

The next morning, Anjali and her mother woke up even earlier than they normally did. It was so early, the scavenging crows hadn't even started their morning screeching as they fought with one another and any other bird that came near them.

Ma was so struck by what Keshavji had said, about how the Dalits didn't need saving, but rather everyone else did, she was determined to start making a change to better themselves. She and Anjali were going to start cleaning their own outhouse so Mohan would no longer have to.

Dressed in the oldest of their khadi outfits, Anjali and her mother stood before the outhouse. "Ready?" Anjali's mother asked.

Anjali nodded. She followed her mother to the back of the slender concrete outhouse, swatting at some mosquitoes along the way.

"You know, Anju, Gandhiji has cleaned the waste out of toilets before. Several times."

Anjali nodded, afraid she might throw up at the thought of what they were about to do, if she opened her mouth to speak.

"In fact, before he was imprisoned, he used to make all new inhabitants at his ashrams clean the latrines as their first job."

Ma paused at the back of the outhouse. There, behind the vines and creepers that fought for space on the outhouse walls, was an opening.

"Now we just have to take the container out, put it in the wagon, and then walk it to the field. Okay?" Anjali's mother looked a little unsure herself.

Anjali tried to steady her already queasy stomach and reminded herself she was lucky she was going to be carrying the waste in a wagon, rather than carrying the container on her head, the way the Dalits had to for so many years, exposing them to not only the filth of what they were carrying but also to all sorts of bacteria and diseases.

Anjali's mother bent down near the opening, reached into the dark space, and pulled out a rectangular metal container of waste. Although Ma quickly slid the metal lid over the container, the rank smell of a day's worth of human waste from Anjali's family still engulfed the air.

And that was all it took to send Anjali racing away from the outhouse, gagging. She ducked behind the neem tree, her stomach convulsing as she threw up.

She stood up, fighting back tears. How could she do this? This had to be the most repulsive job out there. Why couldn't they just pay someone else to do this job? Someone who voluntarily wanted to do this, unlike the Dalits?

The Dalits. Anjali felt ashamed of herself. Here she was getting so upset when she had a choice in the matter. The Dalits who cleaned toilets had been doing this revolting job for years, a job their ancestors had been stuck doing for centuries, many getting sick and dying from diseases because of it. How was that fair? Mohan had cried to his mother to escape this life, but she'd told him he had no choice. How was that just?

Anjali reached for the jasmine plant near the neem. She held a branch of the fragrant flowers to her nose, trying to forget the sickening stench. But then she remembered Ma was doing it all by herself.

Anjali broke off one jasmine blosson to take along, then headed back to the outhouse. She made sure not to look at the open container lying on the ground. But where was Ma?

Was she disappointed in me for being so weak? Did she go inside to get Baba to help her instead? Anjali wondered. Then she heard a faint moaning.

Anjali peeked around the corner. There at the side of the yard near their guava tree was her mother, bent over sick.

"Ma?" Anjali approached slowly.

Anjali's mother turned to her, face pale, cheeks stained with tears.

"Are you okay?"

Anjali's mother nodded, leaning on the trunk. "This is nauseating work."

"Yes," said Anjali, briefly hoping her mother would change her mind about having them do it.

"Remember that poor baby outside the basti? He didn't have clothes. And I burned so many clothes. Your father told me it was silly. But I didn't listen. I was too busy making a symbolic change, I didn't realize I could have made a real difference for people. Maybe . . . maybe Chachaji was right. I get so caught up in trying to make a change, I don't think it through."

Anjali hated seeing the self-doubt in her mother's once-fearless eyes. "It's just garbage," she said indifferently, even though she was fighting the urge to vomit again. "What are we afraid of?"

"Well, it stinks, for one thing," said Ma.

Anjali smiled. "Yes. It does. So let's get it out of here. If Gandhiji can clean his own toilets at his ashram, so can we."

The color returned to Ma's face as she steadied herself on her feet. "You're right." She nodded, backing away from the tree. "Let's wash up, and then I think I have something that can help."

Anjali and her mother pumped themselves some clean water from the front yard and washed off, and then Ma dashed inside the bungalow and emerged with an old sheer scarf. She tore it in half and handed one piece to Anjali.

"Tie it like this," said Ma, tying the scarf over the lower half of her face so that her nose was totally covered but she could still take in air through the thin fabric.

Anjali followed her mother's lead, tying her scarf in place.

"Now let's try this again, shall we?" And Ma and Anjali once again went to the backyard, to the container of waste.

Anjali could still smell a faint whiff of the container's contents, but she made sure not to look at it or think about it. Making eye contact only with her mother, Anjali helped Ma lift the container into the wagon that stood waiting nearby.

Then Anjali and her mother untied the scarves from their faces and pushed the wobbly wagon over the dirt, across the yard, and through the front gate.

Anjali was grateful it was still early enough that only a few people were walking on the street. They didn't take a second glance at the wagon to see what was being lugged around. In fact, most didn't even look at Anjali or her mother.

But suddenly a voice called to them from behind. "What are you doing?"

Anjali turned in front of her house. It was Mohan. He was leaving one of their neighbors' houses with with a large metal container on his head.

"Mohan? What are *you* doing?" asked Anjali's

mother. "I told you, you don't have to clean toilets anymore."

Mohan paused, briefly looking like he didn't know if he wanted to smile or leave his mouth hanging open in shock. "Just because you told me I don't have to doesn't mean all your neighbors did."

Anjali's mother shook her head. "Of course. How foolish of me."

"And I need to earn a living. I need to eat. I can't do that with some made-up job that doesn't exist for a person like me. I don't have a mother or father looking out for me like some people do."

Anjali's brow furrowed. Was that directed at her? Even though she knew it was wrong, she couldn't help but feel like Mohan found her ideas to be unworthy because they were coming from someone who lived a different life than he did.

"You're absolutely right," Ma said. "I'm so sorry. I guess sometimes we get carried away and don't think things through."

Frustrated, Anjali gripped the wagon handle tighter. Ma didn't need to apologize so much. They were trying, weren't they? How many other Brahmins would clean out their sewage containers like this? Yet if others did pitch in and do their share, would that mean Mohan would starve?

It was wrong to make Mohan do this job. He should be able to do any other work he wanted to do. But it was also wrong to take away Mohan's income before he could learn to read and write or find a profession he liked and was good at, wasn't it?

Anjali couldn't figure out the answers to her questions and felt even more confused than before.

"Maybe we could give you a different job at home. Maybe you could work in our garden." Anjali turned to Ma. "Or do you think Chachaji would get too upset?" She glanced at Mohan, hoping she hadn't offended him. "Not that you being in our garden would ruin it. I just meant—sorry." Anjali pushed her weight into the wagon, wishing she could take her words back.

But Mohan's face softened as he watched Anjali struggle. "Do you know the way to the field?"

Ma nodded. "I think so."

"I have to drop this off. I'll walk with you. If that's okay."

"Of course it is," said Anjali, and the trio started to walk side by side in the direction of Lakshmi Auntie's house, where a milkman was standing before the gate.

The gate opened, and out stepped Suman to pay the milkman for a bottle of milk, since they didn't have their own cow.

Anjali looked down, wishing she could just disappear.

Mohan reached for Anjali's side of the handle. "Give me the wagon."

"Don't be silly, Mohan," said Ma.

"Let me push it until we pass her," he whispered to Anjali.

Anjali's nerves fluttered like a fragile plumeria flower in the rain.

"Before she sees you," added Mohan.

As Suman turned back to her house with the milk, Anjali gave up her handle of the wagon to Mohan, stepping back as Mohan and Ma pushed the rickety wagon together.

Suman's and Anjali's eyes briefly met. Anjali looked away, not sure if she was more embarrassed by what she was almost spotted doing, or by how quickly she gave up the job of pushing her own waste to Mohan.

With Suman now inside her house, Anjali caught up with her mother and Mohan and tried to take the wagon handle again. But Mohan said he didn't mind pushing it up to the field, and Anjali didn't protest too much.

He's older than me, stronger than me, she reasoned, trying hard to convince herself that letting Mohan continue to do this work was okay. *He knows the way. And then I can help on the way home.*

They turned down an alley and headed down a twisting downhill lane until they reached a tiny creek that swirled around lush green fields of spinach at the edge of town. A couple old women, a handful of young children, and a few scrawny men were emptying their containers of feces in a field and then using a little shovel to scrape clumps of dirt over the waste, creating fertilizer.

That means this disgusting stew of excrement was what these plants were nourished with? Anjali gagged at the revolting thought. She watched as Mohan dumped the contents of his container, buried them with a shovel, and then washed the metal container with some creek water nearby.

Ma struggled to lift their container off the wagon. Anjali didn't budge an inch to help her. How could she? Her mind was too busy conjuring up the most sickening images of spinach leaves full of waste.

Mohan rushed to help Ma, and together they dumped the waste out.

I have to help, thought Anjali. But she was so repulsed by the smells and sights, she couldn't get her feet to move as Ma used Mohan's shovel to throw soil over the waste, her sandals turning brown from what Anjali could only hope was soil and not excrement.

Ma washed the container out in the dirty puddle of a creek, put it back in her wagon, and then turned to Anjali. "Ready to head back? You don't want to be late for school. You still need to bathe."

A whiff of fresh air tickled Anjali's nose, thanks to a brief breeze. She couldn't wait to get away from the sewage. With the outhouse container now empty and washed, she snuck a peek at it and actually didn't gag. She took a deep breath and helped her mother push the wagon away from the farm, groaning as she struggled to push the load uphill.

"I know," said her mother, gritting her teeth. "This isn't easy. But I'm proud of you, Anju."

Anjali didn't know what her mother was proud of. She hadn't pushed the wagon to the farm. She hadn't emptied the container. And she hadn't washed it. She was too sickened by it all.

Finally, they made it up the hill. Mohan was right beside them, easily heading up the hill he was so used to climbing.

"You've done more than enough, Mohan," said Ma. "You don't need to help us home."

Mohan again gave Anjali and her mother an amused look. "I have lots more toilets to clean on your street," he answered.

"Oh," said Ma. "Of course."

Anjali felt awful. Here she was making such a big deal out of having to clean her *own* waste and push the wagon to the field, when poor Mohan had to do this all day, every day, carrying loads of other people's sewage, with no say in the matter.

Anjali didn't say anything on the way home. She was too busy feeling bad about her behavior. As they turned onto their street with the wagon, Anjali saw Mangala and Suman chatting outside Mangala's house, dressed in their school uniforms.

"I'll take it," said Mohan, reaching once again for the wagon handle.

Anjali started to let go but then stopped herself. Why was she ashamed to clean up after herself? Why did she feel embarrassed doing something that

Gandhiji had been trying to teach the country about for so long? Something that would free countless people and improve hygiene for so many, saving them from dying from preventable illnesses? Why did she feel humiliated helping her mother with such a great idea? And worst of all, why was she so okay with letting Mohan hold the wagon and continue to be isolated and considered unclean?

She had to change her own attitude before some-one like Suman would change hers. Anjali reminded herself she was the daughter of a freedom fighter. She thought about how bravely her mother had stood up to Captain Brent, to Chachaji, to anyone who tried to tell her that her ideas were foolish.

"They're going to see you," warned Mohan.

"Let them," said Anjali, holding her head up.

Mangala's glance fell on the empty container in the wagon. She gasped as she realized what it was.

"Good morning," Anjali said, holding her head up high. "Just coming back from the field. We cleaned our toilet."

Suman's face turned pale as Anjali passed with the wagon and looked her right in the eyes. Anjali smiled. "See you in school."

CHAPTER 16

After weeks of helping her mother clean the outhouse, Anjali felt stronger. And it wasn't just from all those uphill trips back home from the spinach field. Although she had yet to get used to the awful smell involved with human sewage, Anjali was getting better at hiding her revulsion. Her neighbors and classmates, on the other hand, were having more trouble. Lakshmi Auntie's nostrils would involuntarily flare whenever she saw Ma. Suman and Mangala made sure to never let their lunch tiffins touch Anjali's. But it didn't matter to Anjali because she felt like her mother's plan to help educate the children in the basti was actually working.

Paro was quick at learning her numbers, and Anjali had started to teach her letters. Even though he still thought it wouldn't do much good, Mohan dropped in on lessons whenever he wasn't working, and was starting to write whole words and read short books. Although they still had awkward moments, Anjali had made a few other friends among the children in the basti. She and Rohit would run down the street together to see who was fastest. Urmila and Jyoti were great singers, and Anjali loved to hear them perform. And little Vijay was a really good mimicker, cracking Anjali up with his impressions of the other children, Masterji, and even Ma.

In fact, Anjali liked spending afternoons with her new friends so much, it made her long days at school seem even longer. The January breeze made the warm afternoons a lot more tolerable, but she was more anxious than ever for school to let out so she could see Paro, Rohit, Urmila, Jyoti, Vijay, and the others.

At Pragati, she would hurry to write down the equations Masterji taught the class, then read the passages in the English texts they were learning as fast as she could, and gulp down the chapati and vegetables her mother sent for lunch in her brass tiffin container every day, but none of that did anything to help school go by faster.

As school got out that afternoon, Anjali and Irfaan rushed out the door, breezing past Anasuya and Nirmala, when Anjali paused. Both those girls knew what it was like to have a family member in the freedom struggle. Maybe they too would enjoy helping out in the basti.

Anjali called out to her two classmates. "We're going to tutor the Dalits this afternoon. Want to join us?"

"Who are the Dalits?" Anasuya asked.

"The children in the basti down the street," replied Anjali.

"The Untouchables?" squealed Nirmala.

Anasuya shook her head. "Ma doesn't like me doing anything after school. I have to go straight home and study."

Anjali remembered how stressed out and angry Anasuya's mother was.

"But don't you want to do your part?" Anjali asked, trying to keep up with the girls.

"You're as crazy as your mother," Nirmala uttered, walking faster to join Suman and Mangala and whispering to them as they headed outside.

"What about you, Anasuya? Your father is a freedom fighter. He must have taught you about Dalits and the vision of the future of India without people being considered Untouchable."

Anasuya just shook her head. "I have to go." She ran down the street toward her house.

Anjali didn't get it. Maybe Nirmala was too far removed from the freedom movement since it was her uncle and not her mother or father who was a freedom fighter, but Anasuya's own father was working every day for India's independence. He must have been aware that equality for all would make Indians stronger against the British. Sure, Anasuya was a Brahmin, but why would she be so scared of helping the Dalits?

As Anjali and Irfaan headed out, she stopped frowning. There by the peepal tree stood her father, handing a few coins to a white-haired beggar who was hunched over with age, her old sari full of holes. The beggar cupped the coins in her wrinkled hand and touched her forehead with it to show her gratitude before hobbling away.

"Baba! What are you doing here?"

Anjali's father smiled. "Classes got out early today, so I thought I'd come help you and Ma. Why do you look so down?"

"She asked Nirmala and Anasuya to help us today,"

said Irfaan as they walked down the hill. "Anasuya seemed scared, and Nirmala . . . well, she was Nirmala. She seemed sick at the thought of the Dalits."

"Well, everyone has their own opinions. From what I remember, you two were a little nervous at first about working in the basti too," said Anjali's father. "This reminds me of Akbar and Birbal."

Anjali shared a small smile with Irfaan. He had probably heard Baba's Birbal stories almost as much as Anjali, given the amount of time the friends spent together at Anjali's house.

Baba began his tale. "One day Emperor Akbar was bragging to Birbal about how loyal his subjects were. To prove it, he decided to fill the palace pool with milk so that he could take a milk bath. He told everyone in his kingdom to show their dedication to him by bringing one pitcher of milk each to pour into the pool that night. But milk was expensive. One man thought, 'I'll just bring a pitcher of water. With everyone else bringing milk, the emperor will not know I cheated.' But it turned out, every single subject thought the same as that man. No one did what needed to be done, and the next morning poor Emperor Akbar was left—"

"—with a pool of water," finished Anjali.

Baba nodded. "That's right."

"What does that have to do with Nirmala and Anasuya?" asked Anjali.

"In order for Dalit people to finally be free of centuries of stigma, everyone must pitch in. Those girls will come around one day, I hope. In the meanwhile, you and Irfaan continue to pour those pitchers of milk in, and before you know it, the pool will be full."

Inside the basti, as Masterji started writing letters on the chalkboard in preparation for the afternoon's lesson and Ma set up the little chalkboards on the ground near the garden, Baba, Anjali, Paro, Mohan, and Irfaan played gilli danda nearby. Kavita, Jyoti, and Dinanath were watching and applauding anytime someone played well.

Anjali whipped the gilli as hard as she could with the danda. It went flying over Irfaan's head, past little Paro, out of Baba's reach, and out of the basti.

"Oops," said Anjali with a shrug as the young children around her doubled over in laughter. In the several weeks she had spent with her new friends, they certainly were getting comfortable around her. Comfortable enough to laugh with her, and even laugh at her.

Paro, Anjali, and Irfaan rushed outside to find the gilli had landed right in the middle of a pile of purple eggplants on a vegetable vendor's cart. Unfortunately for them, the grocer's face was quickly turning the same color as the eggplants. "It's ruined. It's all ruined!" the man shouted.

Irfaan slowed down, not one to head for conflict.

"Come on," muttered Anjali, dragging him with her as Mohan watched from the basti, Anjali's danda in hand. Paro slowed, trailing behind Anjali and Irfaan. "Sorry, Uncle," Anjali said to the grocer. "I didn't mean to hit it so hard."

"You? Anjali? You're playing with those Untouchables?" he shrieked, his voice rising as he pointed to Paro. "What will your parents think?"

Paro looked down nervously as Mohan walked up, protectively putting his arm around her.

"My parents know I'm playing there," said Anjali. "They're just people, Uncle. Your vegetables are fine. Nothing's ruined."

The man's color returned to normal on his leathery skin, burned from working all day in the sun. "Nobody saw it, so this time it's okay," he muttered, glancing around the street.

A flush of heat rushed to Anjali's cheeks. This man had no right to judge. He had no idea how Mohan struggled every day. He didn't know what kind of jobs Dalits had to do in order to survive. *And I bet he has no clue that some of his spinach was probably grown with the help of the fertilizer made at the farm.* Anjali smiled, imagining his face if he were to ever put two and two together.

"If any of my customers were to see a filthy Untouchable's toy land in their food . . . I can't even think of what would happen to my business." The grocer shuddered.

Anjali rolled her eyes. "You should call them Dalits. Not Untouchables." She grabbed the gilli off the cart and tossed it to Mohan. "You'll see, Uncle. One day all these thoughts will be outdated, and India will finally be free."

The man shook his head. "You should spend less time here and more time over there in school, beta," he said, pointing to Pragati down the road. "Your mind is getting dulled by your dirty surroundings."

Anjali was getting sick of others acting this way to Mohan, Paro, and the others. It was bad enough to see Anasuya and Nirmala terrified and repulsed by them, unable to understand they were all people, but to see a grown man act this way made Anjali's pulse beat angrily in her ears. "You're right, Uncle," she fumed as Irfaan pleaded with his eyes for her to stop raising her voice at an elder. "You're absolutely right. I should spend more time at school. In fact, all of us kids should. It seems pretty silly teaching the kids here when there's a perfectly good school just down the street."

The grocer stared at Anjali for a second. Then he muttered a prayer under his breath and pushed his cart away.

Mohan and Paro ran to Anjali's and Irfaan's side. "I've never seen anyone talk to an elder like that, Brahmin or otherwise," said Mohan. "You really might be crazy."

Anjali gave Mohan an offended look.

"Sorry. I overheard your neighbor say that about you when I was cleaning her toilet."

Anjali sighed. There was no escaping Suman and her comments.

Irfaan lowered his voice. "Were you serious about what you said back there?"

"Very." Anjali stood firm. "What's the point of a school called Pragati if there isn't any progress? We have students of different religions and castes at our school. But no Dalit students? Well, it's time for some change. Time for some real progress. Paro is going to go to school with us. I'm going to make sure of it."

She turned to Mohan. "Will you join us? I know an education won't earn you money right away, but maybe we can provide your meals so you can go. Or maybe find you another job you can do in the evenings after school. I really don't care if Chachaji is upset with you being our gardener. I'll talk to Baba about it right now. Or maybe—"

"I'll join you," interrupted Mohan, smiling reassuringly at Paro as the grocer faded into the background the farther away he pushed his cart. "Now come on. Let's get back to our game. I have a strange feeling we might actually win," he added, tossing Anjali the danda.

CHAPTER 17

$\mathcal{M}$asterji and Anjali's mother loved Anjali's idea and set about implementing it over the next few weeks. But not everyone else was so enthusiastic about the change.

The vegetable vendor stopped going to their house. Anjali's mother had to walk a few neighborhoods down to find a grocer who didn't know who she was, and therefore wasn't afraid she would taint the goods because she associated with Dalits. Chachaji was so shocked by what his family members were trying to do that he barely spoke to them anymore. Instead he just grunted and huffed angrily whenever Anjali or Ma tried to speak to him. Anjali was so fed up with his childish behavior, she didn't even bother saying bye to him when she left for school in the morning, and she certainly did not bow down to him anymore.

That afternoon, when Anjali, Irfaan, Ma, and Masterji were leaving the basti, they were confronted by Lakshmi Auntie, Suman, and a handful of angry neighbors in the street.

"Who do you think you are, changing our school without our approval?" barked Lakshmi Auntie, proving to be not nearly as sweet as Anjali once thought.

"Some schools in bigger cities opened their doors to Dalit children years ago," Ma replied.

"They don't need to learn. What will they do with that knowledge?" snapped Mangala's mother, a member of the trader caste who owned a pottery store nearby. "You'd understand that if you understood how the real world works. Not everyone is born with a silver spoon in their mouth." She eyed Ma's sparkling diamond earrings.

Anjali's mother shook her head. "Everyone thinks I'm so privileged. You know how I first learned English?"

"A private tutor?" retorted Mangala's mother.

"That's right."

Mangala's mother scoffed.

"But the tutor wasn't for me. He was for my brother. I wanted to learn too, but my parents said, 'What use is English to a girl?' and made me work in the kitchen instead. I went to the kitchen. And I worked there. But as I was cutting vegetables and kneading dough, I was listening. Because my brother was learning English in the room next door. *That's* how I learned. And that's when I decided a woman can do anything a man can do. Knowledge is important. And it should be accessible to *everyone*."

"Drop this plan now, Masterji," said Lakshmi Auntie, ignoring Ma. "Or we'll take our tuition money elsewhere."

Anjali watched as Suman's lips turned upward in a haughty smile.

"Where will you go?" Anjali asked Suman. "To St. Xavier's on the other end of town? It's near the college. With all those professors' children going to school with you, you may not be first in class anymore. But suit yourself."

Suman's arrogant grin briefly shrunk, but in a blink, she was right back to her old smirking self. "You're a professor's child. I don't have any trouble beating your marks."

"Take the risk, then," retorted Anjali. "I hope you're right."

Suman gave her mother's bangles a tiny tug with her finger. Lakshmi Auntie turned to her. The bells on Suman's earrings jingled ever so slightly as she subtly shook her head, pleading with her mother.

Lakshmi Auntie sighed. "Fine. We'll stay."

"And the children from the basti?" asked Masterji.

"They can come."

The other parents gasped.

"But they can only sit in the back. And they better not sit anywhere near my Suman," she snapped. She clutched Suman's hand and stormed off.

The other parents looked momentarily confused.

"They can't be near Mangala, either!" huffed Mangala's mother.

"Or Ravi," said another mother, as more and more parents shouted their children's names at Ma and Masterji before hurrying after Lakshmi Auntie.

"Wait," Anjali called out in vain. But no one was listening. "How is that showing we're all equal? Paro and Mohan and everyone should be able to sit with everyone else."

Masterji watched the angry parents heading down

the street. "It's a start, Anjali. We'll change their minds yet."

Anjali looked at the hopeful glimmer in Masterji's and Ma's eyes. But no matter how hard she tried to convince herself it would all work out, no matter how hard she tried to have her own eyes fill with hope, they just kept filling with tears.

That evening, Anjali and Ma found Mohan helping Paro with their tiny garden. Mohan was clearing some weeds and stones while Paro watered each plant tenderly. Sunbeams fell this way and that on the collection of herbs, casting all sorts of shadows.

"We are all set for you to start school next week," Ma said softly to Mohan. "There's just one thing . . ."

Anjali cleared her throat. "The other parents will leave if you don't sit in the back."

Mohan swiped at the dirt, clearing some pebbles.

"I'm sorry," Anjali said. "I don't think it's fair, either."

"It's not forever. We'll change their minds. Masterji is sure of it." Ma fiddled with her bangles, sliding them back and forth between her fingers. "It's still a big step.

It's like your garden. The sun still reaches the plants at the back, right?" she said, pointing to the little herbs at the back of the basti garden.

Mohan shrugged. "Sometimes. And sometimes the plants in the back never even rise out of the dirt. Because their world is just full of too many weeds."

CHAPTER 18

*A*njali couldn't stop thinking about how unfair it was to force Mohan, Paro, Urmila, Dinanath, Suraj, and the other children to sit in the back of the classroom. And based on the number of dirty looks Suman had given Anjali over the course of the rest of the week, Anjali wasn't sure her classmates would ever be okay with the upcoming change, either.

But it wasn't all bad.

Jamuna told Ma she was proud to be working for their family. Farhan Uncle, Irfaan's father, donated notebooks and pencils for the new students. Keshavji paid for Paro's and the other children's textbooks and agreed to cover Mohan's meals so he could give up cleaning toilets to go to school. And the Khadi Shop tailors sewed the children some uniforms for school, all free of charge.

Anjali couldn't help but have a huge smile on her face as she and Irfaan walked home from school that Saturday afternoon, down the big hill and past the peepal tree. Tomorrow, school would be off, and then on Monday, Paro, Mohan, and the others would finally get to come to Pragati. She couldn't wait.

"You're going to ruin everything, Anjali!" shouted Suman from behind as they turned the corner, passing Captain Brent's bungalow.

"Ignore her," whispered Irfaan.

But Anjali yelled back, "And just what am I going to ruin?"

"It's not going to be fun to go to school anymore!" Suman ran tearfully away as Nirmala and Mangala neared, glaring at Anjali.

"What?" Anjali snapped. "Am I ruining something for you too?"

"Not something, everything," Nirmala retorted. "Thanks to your foolish plan."

"Foolish?" Anjali repeated. "Your uncle was a freedom fighter."

"Yes, and he was foolish, too, and lost his life. That's

why my father always tells me to stay away from you freedom fighters. You have ridiculous ideas about changing things that haven't changed for centuries. You don't think about the consequences of your actions."

Mangala nodded. "She's right. And who knows what worse fate will happen to the unfortunate kids who have to sit on the bench next to those Untouchables?"

"I'll happily sit in the back," Anjali said.

"Me too," said Irfaan.

"They're no different than us," Anjali argued. "And they're my friends. Our friends," she added, including Irfaan.

"You're right. You've been visiting them, so you're *all* unclean. So you're *all* the same," said Mangala, waving at both Anjali and Irfaan.

The girls turned their noses up as they breezed by.

"Don't worry about them," said Irfaan as he and Anjali entered the small kitchenware shop near their school. "They don't know what they're talking about."

Anjali tried not to think of her current classmates and focus instead on her future ones as she and Irfaan neared the back counter. Several freedom fighters had managed to get enough donations to purchase small tiffin containers for each Dalit student, so that they would have something to keep their meals in, just like the other students did.

Anjali greeted the potbellied owner of the store, who looked like he rarely smiled. "Hello, Raju Uncle. Are the tiffin containers ready to be picked up?"

The man nodded to the stack of containers on the counter.

Anjali began to fill her jute bag with them. She turned to Irfaan. "Aren't you going to help me?"

"Abbu wanted me to get a new pitcher for home," he said, pointing to a medium-sized stainless steel jug on a shelf on the opposite wall. "I'll take that one, Uncle." Irfaan handed the shopkeeper some money. "And could you please engrave 'Farhan Ansari' on it?" asked Irfaan, spelling his father's name.

"What's the point?" asked the grumpy man.

Anjali took a step closer to Irfaan, who looked taken aback. "The point is so he knows which container is his family's. Why does anyone get their dishes engraved?"

The man bared his decaying teeth at Anjali. "I mean, what's the point of engraving his name on it when his people want to leave our land. Haven't you heard? The Muslims want their own country, where no Hindus are allowed. When the time comes, your friend and his family will have to rush to leave."

Anjali's stomach felt queasy. She had heard murmurings of some Muslims wanting this. Some Muslim leaders felt Muslims would be safer there when the British finally gave up their claim to India. But it wasn't what Gandhi wanted. *And it certainly isn't what Irfaan wants*, Anjali thought as the shopkeeper continued, leaning closer to Irfaan.

"You think you will have time to take all your belongings? Every bowl and cup? Leave it blank. Then some good Hindu family will be able to use it when you leave."

Tears rushed to Irfaan's eyes.

Anjali fumed. "He paid for it. So just do it. Put Farhan Uncle's name on it, and we will leave."

The shopkeeper glared, carelessly etching the pitcher with Irfaan's dad's name and brusquely sliding the container down the counter to the kids.

Anjali opened her mouth to say more to the rude man, but Irfaan just pulled her out of the shop, his face burning red. "Let it be."

Anjali shook her head. "But—"

"I said let it be!" Irfaan quickly softened. "It's fine.

Really. See you tonight at Victoria Garden. Okay?" Irfaan turned and ran down the winding street to his neighborhood, but not before Anjali saw a couple tears spill down his cheeks.

Anjali walked home, feeling uneasy. Why was Raju Uncle so mean to Irfaan? And why couldn't her classmates see that Mohan or Paro were no different from them? Other castes were shunning Dalits, Hindus and Muslims were fighting again, and the British were still just as strong as ever. Was anything ever going to get better? Was everything going to be okay on Monday when Paro and Mohan joined her school? And would they ever get to really be treated as equals, and not forced to sit in the back of the classroom?

Anjali tried to shake the bad feeling she was getting. Going to Victoria Garden tonight to check out the fair was just what she needed to calm her nerves. She couldn't wait to see all the beautiful beaded purses and mirrored sashes that would be sold there. And she hoped Mohan would be there too, selling his necklaces.

She opened the gate to her compound. Her mother was holding a wooden stick above her head, using it to take the stiff, starched clothes off the high line on the porch. Anjali's father and Chachaji were nearby, examining the garden, eyebrows wrinkled.

"What's going on?" asked Anjali.

"Looks like the methi plants won't make it." Anjali's father sighed. "They just weren't strong enough to fight the disease."

Anjali glanced at the withered plants, their clusters of oblong lime green leaves now just shriveled brown twists. "No more of Jamuna's methi paratha," she said sadly, thinking of her favorite lunch of hot flatbread tinted green from the bitter leaves.

Chachaji clicked his tongue, speaking more than he had in weeks. "It's an omen. You must've touched the plants after playing with those dirty Untouchables."

"Chachaji," said Anjali's father.

"Why do you think these bad things are happening? Anjali and her mother are polluting our caste. They're bringing bad luck to our family."

"If I didn't have to teach at the college to support us, I would be right by their side, helping them," Anjali's father retorted.

The faint dinging of a bicycle bell cut the tension as the postman pulled to a stop in front of their gate.

Anjali's father went to greet him. "Why so late, Ramu?" he asked.

The postman handed Baba a few letters, speaking in a low tone so Anjali could only hear a few stray words.

"There's trouble, sahib. Big trouble in the city . . . Riots. Hindu-Muslim riots . . . Not to be trusted . . . Make sure you lock up the gates tonight." And with those ominous words, the postman left.

"What did he mean, 'Hindu-Muslim riots'?" asked Anjali, worry creasing her brow as she rememebered that communal riots had made Chachaji lose his home. "Are we rioting together against the British?" She feared the answer was really that the Hindus and Muslims were arguing about the country some Muslims wanted for themselves. "What about ahimsa?"

Anjali's father smiled. "It's nothing, Anju. Why don't you and Ma read this letter? It's from Suresh Mama."

"Yes, Anjali. Let's see what he has to say," Ma said cheerfully.

A bit too cheerfully.

Anjali knew her parents were trying to distract her, and she wasn't going to fall for it, even though she was excited to see what her mother's brother had to say. He lived all the way on the eastern side of the country, in Bengal.

She tore open the thin paper envelope to find the letter inside. She was careful to hold the edges of it so the blue ink her uncle had written with wouldn't smudge.

"'Dear Shailaja,'" read Anjali, "'we are all safe, yet I'm afraid these are troubling times for India. There are riots here every day. I've witnessed Hindu and Muslim brothers fighting as enemies, and it sickens my heart. There is so much bloodshed here, and the British just sit back and enjoy it as we fight amongst ourselves like fools. Sometimes I fear for my life, but I pray things will be better. Take care of yourself and be safe. With love, Suresh.'"

Anjali looked up from the letter to see stunned looks on the faces of her parents and Chachaji. She knew Hindu-Muslim riots had forced Chachaji out of his home two years ago. But she wasn't clear what exactly a riot entailed.

"What does it mean?" she asked, feeling a nervous fluttering in her chest.

"Nothing," said Anjali's mother, snatching the letter from Anjali's hands.

"What about school on Monday? And the tiffin containers?" Anjali held up her jute bag, the metal containers clanging together. "I have theirs. You were going to give these to them tonight before the fair."

"Let's all go inside," said Anjali's mom, forcing a smile.

"But—"

"Come." Anjali's father gently led her inside before rushing back out to lock the iron gate, giving it a forceful tug to make sure it was secure.

That evening, Anjali and her family ate dinner in almost complete silence. The normally cacophonous din of people walking on the street was also strangely muted.

"Shouldn't we turn on the radio? To know what's going on?" asked Chachaji. He fumbled with the dial.

Through the sounds of static, journalists reported chaos in the market, stores being set on fire, vandalism, and theft. A pit formed in Anjali's stomach as if someone were taking a shovel to her insides. "I want to check on Irfaan," she said, her voice shaking.

"You want to get killed?" snapped Chachaji. "And for a Muslim?"

"Chachaji," said Ma sharply. "You have to stop thinking like this. Hindus and Muslims were both at fault for the riots in Bombay." She gave Anjali's hand a squeeze. "He is right about it not being safe, though."

"But we're supposed to go to Victoria Garden tonight for the fair. What if Irfaan's waiting for me there? What if something happens to him?"

"Let him wait. You're not going outside," said Chachaji firmly.

"Baba?" pleaded Anjali, turning to her father.

"Sorry," replied Baba. "I'm sure Farhan Uncle also knows it's not safe and has kept Irfaan at home. No one leaves tonight. That means you too, Jamuna. It's better to be safe than sorry."

The maid shakily nodded.

"Set up a bed in Anjali's room," said Ma, running her fingers across the bars on the windows. The windows in their bungalow had always had bars instead of glass. They allowed fresh air to come in and kept some rain out, although they weren't very successful in keeping sparrows from coming in, and a couple times a day Chachaji would have to shoo away the birds. But now the bars felt strangely like a prison. Anjali's mother closed the shutters on the windows, locking them. "We'll all go to bed early tonight."

Off in the distance, the haunting howls of street dogs swept over Navrangpur with the evening wind.

CHAPTER 19

Anjali followed Jamuna to her bedroom, still unsure of what was going on. What were these riots? Why were Hindus and Muslims fighting against one another? Was it because some people wanted India to be split into two countries? And why couldn't she forget the image of Raju Uncle glaring at Irfaan with eyes full of hatred?

Jamuna opened the mirrored double doors to Anjali's armoire. Looking at the peacocks dancing on the painted door of the armoire gave Anjali no comfort now.

"I knew this would happen," muttered Jamuna as she pulled out some cotton sheets and pillows to place over the thin, dusty striped mattress she had unfolded on the floor. "The Muslims were just waiting for an opportunity to act up."

Anjali's lip quivered. How could Jamuna talk like this? "But, Jamuna, Hindus are equally at fault, aren't they?"

"They're too different from us, Anjali," said Jamuna, tucking the sheets under the mattress.

Anjali knew that Islam and Hinduism were totally unlike each other, but until today, she had never really dwelled on the differences. Hindus believed that there was one God who took millions of different human and animal forms. They worshipped various idols of these different forms in their temples. Muslims also believed that there was one God, but their God had no form and was never depicted as an idol. Many Hindus, like Anjali, were vegetarian and revered cows for all that they did for them: for plowing the fields with their strength, feeding their families with their milk, and giving their dung for fuel. Although Muslims could not eat pork, they were not vegetarian and did eat beef.

But despite all these differences, Hindus and Muslims, for the most part, got along in India. Anjali loved celebrating Eid-al-Fitr after Ramadan with Irfaan and exchanging gifts, and Irfaan always stopped by during Diwali to enjoy the tasty treats Anjali's mother made. It made Anjali sick to think that the two factions were now killing each other.

Her thoughts turned back to Irfaan. What if he were to get hurt?

Anjali looked down at the floor, where the exhausted maid was nestled into her makeshift bed. Within seconds, a throaty snoring emitted from Jamuna's nose.

While Jamuna's nostrils flared away, Anjali gripped her gold bangles together, silencing them as she slid them over her wrist and off her hand. She pinched the hooks on her silver anklets, unlatching them and their noisy bells, and placed the jewelry gently on her cotton bedsheet. Covering all sources of noise she could possibly make, Anjali tiptoed around Jamuna and slipped out her bedroom door.

The main hall was deserted, and the slate tiles felt unusually cold to Anjali's feet. She fought back a shiver and quietly made her way out the hall, past her parents' bedroom, and past Chachaji's room, until she reached the back doors that led to the patio.

Anjali put her sandals on and quietly unhooked the rusty upper latch on one of the doors. She slowly shifted the bolt in the middle of the doors until it unlatched, and snuck out.

The night air smelled strange. It was heavily masked by the smell of smoke and made Anjali's throat and ears itch inside. She jumped down the patio steps, and passed Nandini's shed. The cow was fast asleep.

Despite the nervous feeling clawing at her insides, Anjali headed up the small hill to the outhouse, put her left foot in the hole in the back wall, and, with her right foot, used the trunk of the neem tree to boost herself over the crumbling concrete barrier and into the dirt alley below.

Anjali was now outside the protection of her compound, but she had to make sure her friend was okay. She had to know Irfaan wasn't still waiting for her at the Victoria Garden. She snuck through the back passage, traveling between the other houses in Madhuban Colony. It was strange to see them all quiet and dark this early in the moonless night. Everyone seemed to have gone to bed early, like her family. Anjali guessed the postman's warning had spread, but it only served to make the eerily hushed streets scary.

The only sounds she could hear, the chirping crickets and the unknown hisses of reptiles in the shadows, did not make the environment any friendlier. Anjali hurried through the alley, hoping not to step on any bugs, praying she wouldn't encounter any scorpions, and exited out of a clearing onto the main road and the shops ahead. There were a sari shop, a jewelry store, a cobbler's hut, a shoe store, and a tailor's tiny shack, all scattered along a dusty, neem tree–lined lane.

The street was deserted except for three sleeping goats. The two white goats and the little brown goat were tied with rope to a post in front of the shoe store. Anjali took a deep breath, reminding herself that she had traveled down this street countless times in her life in the daytime, and headed in the direction of Victoria Garden.

When a man's agonized screams pierced the air, Anjali froze.

The goats stood up and bleated, a look of alarm in their widening eyes. After a few heartbeats, Anjali ducked behind a stinking pile of trash on the side of the street. Up ahead, the faint glimmer of orange flames could be seen. A group of men charged down the street, torches in hand. But some of them also held knives, machetes, and metal rods.

They pounded on the shoe store next door with

their weapons, shattering the glass. They waved their torches across the storefront, lighting it on fire. The blaze roared as the men continued to shout, their faces dripping with sweat and blinded by rage. The long vermilion marks on their forehead glistened in the ghostly glow. They were Hindu, attacking a business owned by a Muslim family.

The men ran past the goats, who could not escape the heat of the fire. Anjali watched in horror as the flames that ravaged the footwear inside the store crept toward the smallest of the goats. The furry brown animal cowered back, trying in vain to escape, but it was no use—its neck was tied to a post. The goat screamed, a terrible, high-pitched bleat.

Just then, around the corner, another group of armed men raced forward. They wore topis, the same skullcaps as Irfaan's cousins, so Anjali knew they were Muslim.

Her heart raced.

Suddenly the two groups spotted each other and charged, shouting, waving their blades into a bloody clash. Anjali suppressed her scream as she caught glimpses of unspeakable violence in the quick flashes of fire.

She wanted to turn back and lock herself in her home, but something about the poor goats pleading for help stopped her. Anjali had to do something. So she closed her eyes, begged the brave goddess Durga to give her strength and protection, and, dodging the brutal horde of fighting men, ran across the street right toward the inferno.

Anjali began to untie the tight knots of rope binding the goats. Her fingers trembled. Her palms were slick with sweat. And the terrified goats pulled back so forcefully, they were unintentionally tying the knots tighter. Anjali struggled with the rope. The brown goat's panicked screams grew louder as it tried desperately to scramble back. The tips of its fur were singed black.

There was no time!

The heat from the fire and the sweat from her nerves made the rope slip repeatedly out of Anjali's grip. She glanced at the fighting just a few dozen feet ahead of her. It looked like she had gone unnoticed, but she still felt unsafe. She crouched around the terrified animals, wiped her sweaty hands on her ghagra, and, mustering all the strength she could find, dug her fingers into the main knot and pulled at it until at last the ropes came free. Suddenly sprung loose, the goats fled down the street.

But their abrupt movement caught the attention of the mob.

"Hey!" shouted nameless voices from the shadows. "Hindu or Muslim?"

Anjali fell back on the ground, her palms scraping on the rocky surface. The heat from the burning store was almost scalding her skin.

A blade was raised in the light. Anjali began to shake. A peppering of fuzzy black spots flashed before her eyes. Just as the knife was about to be lowered, a shrieking whistle pierced the air.

The men froze.

"Leave her alone!" shouted a British voice.

Anjali turned to see Captain Brent standing there as a dozen Indian policemen charged the crowd, rifles in hand.

Captain Brent fired a warning shot from his revolver into the sky. The noise was immediately followed by the startled caws of crows as they flew away in panic. Without giving it a second thought, Anjali ran to Captain Brent and tearfully threw her arms around him.

Captain Brent looked down at Anjali. "Arrest them!" he shouted to the police officers.

Anjali held tightly onto Captain Brent, burying her face in his midsection, as the sounds of scuffling and violence slowly died down.

CHAPTER 20

The whole town was reeling from the rioters' actions the night before. Several dozen people had lost their lives. Temples and mosques had been vandalized, stores had been burned to the ground, and after finding out from Captain Brent that they had almost lost their daughter, Anjali's parents were not letting her out of their sight. Even Chachaji was keeping a watchful eye on Anjali, following her every time she got up from the main hall.

As mildly amusing as it was to see Chachaji struggle to keep up with her, Anjali was tired of just staying at home, listening to all the devastation on the radio. Jamuna had broken down earlier when she heard that her cousin's basti on the far side of town had been set on fire. The news scared Anjali. She wanted to check on everyone at Mohan's basti, and she still wanted to see if Irfaan was okay.

But none of that was okay right now, her parents had told her. It was too dangerous, they said. It was too risky for Ma to venture out to teach anyone how to spin cotton on the charkha or for Baba to go to the college. It wasn't even safe enough to go to the spinach field, so Anjali's parents had resorted to digging a hole in the backyard and burying the contents of the outhouse container there until things calmed down.

Anjali rested on the cool slate tiles, worrying about Irfaan while half-listening to the Hindi songs on the radio with her family. Jamuna squatted inches above the ground to wipe the floor around her with a graying wet rag. Suddenly a man's voice interrupted, announcing the call to prayer from the street behind them, near Irfaan's mosque.

Jamuna squeezed the dirty water into the bucket behind her. "Ridiculous. Why must they force all of us to hear when they need to pray?"

"Jamuna," said Anjali's father sternly.

"Here we go," muttered Chachaji, looking up from

a yellowed book he was reading since the newspaper hadn't come that morning.

"We will not tolerate that kind of talk in our home," continued Anjali's father.

"You heard what they did to my cousin's home," replied Jamuna. "They burned it down, and I don't even know if he is alive . . ." Jamuna trailed off as messy tears sputtered down her face and into the crevices around her nose.

Anjali's mother rushed to Jamuna's side and gave her a hug. "I know, Jamuna. It's hard. I hope he's okay. It's hard to wait and wonder, but we cannot fight amongst ourselves."

Jamuna wailed even louder.

Anjali took advantage of the distraction and slipped out the back door. She felt awful for Jamuna, but she had to make sure Irfaan was alive. If he was, he would pass Anjali's home to get to his mosque. Maybe, just maybe, he'd stop by today, and things could feel like normal. Anjali swiftly raced up the outhouse hill and propped herself up with the hole in the concrete wall.

Just a few feet away, she could see a mass of curls through the leaves of the guava trees in the alley.

"Irfaan!" she shouted with joy.

Irfaan emerged from behind the foliage, a few feet behind his father, but his face didn't have its usual innocent cheer.

Anjali waved excitedly, but he just passed her in silence. "Irfaan. It's me, Anjali," she called out.

Farhan Uncle stopped. "Anjali! I'm so glad you're all right. We're going to check on the mosque. How are your parents?"

"We'll be late for prayers," Irfaan said.

Farhan Uncle's eyes narrowed at Irfaan. "Is your family okay, Anjali?" he asked.

Anjali nodded. "Yes, Uncle. We're all fine."

Farhan Uncle nodded.

"Abbu, you go ahead," Irfaan said, walking toward Anjali's back wall. "I'll be right behind you."

"What's your problem?" Anjali asked, her eyebrows narrowing.

"My problem?" Irfaan said once his father was out of earshot. "What is your people's problem?"

"My people?"

"You Hindus. You attacked all our stores. You tried to burn down the mosque."

Anjali glared at her friend. "Like your people are any better. Didn't you hear the radio this morning? You tried to break the idols at our temple. You threw rocks in our store windows. You almost killed me!"

She knew that was unfair. She didn't know if the man who tried to kill her was Muslim or Hindu but she was furious and terrified, and thinking about her terrifying moment with the mobs made her fight back tears.

"Where's your paintbrush?" Irfaan asked.

"What?"

"Someone wrote, 'Muslims, quit India,' on the front of our dairy."

Anjali was shocked. "And you think I did it? I'd never—"

"Just like you'd never paint a Q on Brent Sahib's bungalow?"

Anjali paused. Had Irfaan forgotten how she had stood up for him with Raju Uncle yesterday? How she had *always* loved him like a brother?

"I'll never talk to you again, Anjali. Never!" shouted Irfaan as he ran down the alley, kicking up swirls of yellow dust.

"Good," retorted Anjali. "Good riddance. You're no brother of mine. I can't wait to wash my hair on Mondays." She watched Irfaan disappear around the corner and hopped down the wall back into her yard. "Who needs him?" she muttered to herself as she entered the cow shed to check on Nandini.

Despite what was coming out of her mouth, Anjali couldn't help but cry for what was happening to her friendship and to her land. She rested her head on Nandini's shoulder for comfort.

The cow rubbed her snout on Anjali's face, wiping her tears.

Right then, Anjali's mother rushed in. "There you are. We were so worried. You can't keep slipping away like this. The most terrible thoughts rush into our heads—"

Anjali turned away from her mother, but it was too late.

"You're crying?"

Anjali shook her head. "I just want to be excited for tomorrow. For Paro and Mohan to come to school. To change minds and let the children sit wherever they want. But instead . . . instead I hate Irfaan, and I hate the Muslims. This is all their fault."

"Anjali," exclaimed her mother, looking pale. "Did you not hear what I *just* said to Jamuna?"

Anjali looked down.

Her mother sat in the straw next to her. She ran her

fingers through Anjali's tear-stained hair, gently moving it out of her sticky face.

"Do you see this grass?" asked Anjali's mother, picking up a handful of the long yellow blades of grass from the wooden feed trough.

Anjali sniffled, nodding.

"Do you see this water?" her mother asked, moving the trough of water closer.

Anjali again nodded, watching as some of the water spilled over the brim.

"Hindus are the grass. Muslims are the water. Mother India needs both to survive," Ma said softly, pointing to the pregnant cow. "If you give her just one," she continued, feeding Nandini grass, "she will still need the other."

Nandini gobbled the grass and bent her head to the trough for a sip.

"But when they fight," stated Anjali's mother, repeatedly offering Nandini the grass and then the water but not letting her have either, "Mother India will perish."

Anjali tensed up as she saw Nandini give up on the food and the water out of frustration and turn her head dejectedly.

"We can't starve our mother. And we must quench her thirst. Understand?" Ma finished as she tenderly gave the hungry, thirsty cow both the grass and the water.

Anjali watched Nandini softly chew the grass and happily drink the refreshing water. The cow looked content, totally unaware that outside the gates of the compound, the world was burning.

CHAPTER 21

By Monday morning, the fires had been put out, but pedestrians were a rare sight. Peacocks were even rarer. Anjali's grandmother used to tell her that peacocks left when times were bad. And times were bad. Other than the occasional barking of fighting street dogs or the chirping of sparrows, the streets were calm and quiet.

Anjali awoke and tried not to think about her fight with Irfaan. She told herself she could make up with him once she saw him in class. He'd have to have come to his senses by now and have realized she would never attack his dairy. Besides, today was the big day. Today was the day Mohan and Paro were going to join her school.

Anjali changed into her uniform right away. Jamuna had set it out for her the day before, when her brothers had come to help her get home safely. They brought word that their cousin was okay despite the fire. The fact that Jamuna needed her family to get her home made Anjali scared for this morning. Scared to go to school after the riots. Scared someone might still be rioting. But her parents had tucked her in the night before and promised her they were going to walk with her to school, to make sure she and the Dalit children were able to attend classes safely.

"Ma? Baba? Are you ready? I'll eat fast, promise." She rushed to the kitchen with a nervous excitement but came to a stop when she saw her parents crouching by the radio. "What is it?"

Baba turned the volume down on the radio, shaking his head. "I'm sorry, Anju. There's a curfew."

"What does that mean?" asked Anjali. "We can't go out after dark, but we can still go to school, right? We have to. The Dalits are going to join us."

"There's no school, Anju," said Baba. "For a week. Not just here. A couple schools in the business district and my college are staying closed for the week too as a precaution."

Anjali sank in her spot. How could this happen? After so much hard work, her friends weren't going to get to go to a real school after all?

Her mother held her hand. "We know how hard you worked for this. And we want them to come to school so badly, but I'm afraid it's going to have to wait until things settle down."

"It's pointless," Anjali said.

Baba scooted closer, drawing Anjali's head onto his shoulder.

"What's the point in trying to get our neighbors to understand that Mohan is our equal, that all Indians are equal," she asked, "when Hindus and Muslims are killing each other outside because each group thinks they're better than the other and no one trusts anyone else? And if we can't even all be equals in each other's eyes, how will we ever work together to defeat the British?"

A banging on the gate interrupted her.

Anjali and her parents tensed up. Baba rushed to the main hall and looked out the barred window beside the door. Anjali watched, staying close to Ma.

"I can't see who it is," whispered Anjali's father, making sure the front door was locked.

Ma nodded. "Everyone to Chachaji's room. It's in the back, so it will be safest if it is rioters. We'll barricade the door with his dresser, and I'll get the chili powder from the masala container."

Anjali looked confused.

"For the rioters' eyes, if they attack. Don't worry, Anju. We are going to be okay. Go."

Anjali's father went to get Chachaji while her mother headed for her collection of spices. Anjali started walking to Chachaji's room, but the clanging on the iron rods outside grew louder.

The cow shed! She had to untie Nandini. She had to give her a chance to escape if the rioters pried open the gate.

The rioters hadn't entered the property yet, so Anjali knew she had time. But she had to be fast. She bolted out the patio doors to the shed in the corner of the yard as the banging on the gate continued. As she fumbled with Nandini's ropes, she caught glimpses of what was on the other side of their front gate.

Anjali stopped. There was a flash of sky blue, which looked familiar. More banging. She moved closer, hiding behind the trunks of the mango trees, until she reached the front yard. There, through the bars, she saw Paro, dressed in the blue school uniform of Pragati.

Anjali breathed easier. "Ma!" she called back to the house. "It's okay. You and Baba can come out."

Her parents rushed out of the house. "What are you doing out here, Anjali?" asked her father, bewildered.

Anjali opened the gate, letting Paro in. Her hair was in perfect plaits, looped and tied with bows on either side of her head, just like the school dress code dictated. She smiled, her eyes brimming with hope and excitement. "Mohan said there's a curfew. He said school was canceled. But I knew he was wrong."

Anjali's heart sank. She looked at her parents helplessly.

"He's not wrong—" Ma ran her fingers along the iron bars, struggling for words. "We're so sorry," she added.

Just then, Anjali caught a figure running in the distance toward them. "Baba!" She pointed. "A rioter?"

Baba started to lock the gate, but as the silhouette grew closer, the tension left Anjali's muscles. It was just Mohan.

"I've been looking everywhere for you!" Mohan said, hands on his knees as he bent over to catch his breath. "Your grandmother was so worried when you ran off."

"You were right," Paro said, tears slipping down her cheeks. "I should have known it wasn't really going to happen."

Ma opened the gate, ushering Mohan inside.

Anjali shook her head. "It is going to happen. Just not now." She bent down and wiped Paro's tears away. "We are all going to school together as soon as this mess is over. I promise."

"I'm not so sure that even your promise can make that dream come true," replied Mohan.

As Baba slammed the gate shut, sliding its lock into place, he gasped.

"What is it?" Ma asked.

He squeaked the iron gate open again. There, at the top of the concrete pillar, was the word *Unclean* dripping down in harsh black paint.

"The rioters . . . they must have painted that last night when we were sleeping," muttered Baba.

Just then, a group of young men ran by. One of them turned to Anjali's mother. Anjali just barely caught his face, obscured as it was by the gate. He looked like Veena Auntie's son. "The Muslims aren't the only ones ruining our traditions," he shouted. "Stop what you're doing. Or we'll stop you." He hurled a stone at the concrete wall that housed the iron gate, just missing Anjali's mother.

"Ma," yelped Anjali.

"It's okay. I'm okay."

Anjali could tell by the way her mother was crossing her arms and rubbing at her elbows that she was shaken up but trying to hide it. Anjali felt ill. Irfaan was mad at her. They couldn't go to school. Then someone vandalized their house. And now a rioter threw a rock at them? What would be next? She remembered the knife being lowered at her the night she freed the goats and trembled.

"Maybe this isn't worth it," Ma said.

Anjali suddenly felt cold and sweaty all at once. "What?"

Ma shrugged. "You're scared. My family shouldn't suffer because of my involvement in the freedom fight. Maybe . . . maybe we should back down. Just for a bit."

Anjali's father put a hand on Ma's back.

Anjali looked at her mother's crestfallen face. The lines on her forehead. The way she was wringing her hands.

Anjali shook her head. "No, Ma."

Her parents turned to her.

"You can't give up."

Anjali's father spoke slowly. "The rioters, they're not thinking straight. They're not acting like decent humans. We almost lost you Saturday night, Anjali."

"Do not ever let someone scare you out of doing what is right," Anjali said. "Remember, Ma? *You* told me that when I was scared of you touching Mohan's broom. And you were right." She turned to her father. "We can't give up, Baba. We have come so far. What if everyone gave up? No one would be left to do the right thing. You'd have a pool of water, not milk."

Baba sighed. "Yes. That may be, but—"

"She's right," said Ma softly.

She straightened up, a look of determination in her eyes. "There's another meeting at the Khadi Shop this afternoon, before the curfew. We're going to keep your promise to Paro. We'll go there together so we can make sure of that."

CHAPTER 22

*D*espite the weekend's riots and the evening curfew and the couple of burned homes they passed on their way, Anjali, Baba, and Ma had dropped Paro and Mohan back at the basti and made it to the Khadi Shop safely. But this meeting was an emergency meeting early in the day. *Perhaps the rioters are saving their worst actions for the night again, once the curfew starts,* Anjali thought as she followed her parents up the shop's twisting stairs until they reached the rickety top floor. The room wasn't as full as usual, with only ten freedom fighters in attendance.

Keshavji stood up in the front. "The riots are spreading. In Bombay the rioters cut telegraph wires, attacked the train stations, killed a conductor, and even burned down a police station, all in the name of fighting the British. Is this what Gandhiji has taught? For us to become monsters?"

"The curfew is making things difficult," said Anjali's mother.

Keshavji nodded. "I know, sister. And we are sorry the school integration in your neighborhood did not happen today. It will happen, though, as soon as things quiet down. That's why it is so important we don't let the curfew stop our progress."

"Isn't there some other location we could hold your school?" asked one of the freedom fighters.

Anjali stood up straighter. Maybe school could still happen this week.

Her mother shook her head. "We could continue to teach them in their own basti. But that defeats the purpose. They are our equals. They have to join our school to make that point clear to everyone else."

Keshavji nodded. "Then as soon as the curfew is lifted, you start the integration. Just be careful. I've heard word that some of the British are afraid what you are doing is going to instigate more violence from certain rioting factions."

Anjali started to feel uneasy again. What kind of

violence? Would they try to hurt Paro or Mohan? Or would they go after Anjali's family? She looked nervously at her mother.

Anjali's mother gave Anjali a reassuring smile. "I'm not afraid of these trumped-up charges. They will use any excuse to get freedom fighters off the street, all to stop us from uniting against them."

Balkishan shouted from the back, "You shouldn't be foolishly brave, Shailajaji. You have to be smart. Someone has already left a warning on your house. I saw it this morning. And now if the British think your actions will worsen the riots, you could be in trouble. We all could be."

"He has a point—we should be careful," said one of the men Anjali had seen with Keshavji at the basti. "My friend in Nagpur has been arrested on trumped-up charges claiming his speech about khadi was inflammatory. Before he even delivered the speech. Can you believe it? But how can we make progress if we don't risk these consequences?"

"You don't want to face the wrath of the rioters," Balkishan continued. "And what if the police show up at the school to stop them? They've done lathi charges all over the north."

Anjali shivered. Lathis were wooden batons that the police carried around to beat people with. During lathi charges, they would beat back whoever they were trying to regain control over, be they rioters or protestors, with those batons. She cringed at the thought of her mother being hit by one as the officers tried to break up a rioting crowd. And the thought of the rioters' cleavers and knives didn't make her feel any better, either.

"It doesn't matter," said her mother. "It doesn't matter if they hit us. Let them. We have strength in numbers. We will just stand there and take the blow. Blow by blow, however bloody it gets, we will not move. We must show them that nonviolence is the way to go. Our school will be integrated. Like Gandhiji said, even a small number of dedicated people can alter the course of history. And alter it we will."

"Hear, hear, sister!" shouted a handful of men and women from the group.

The rest of the meeting seemed to take forever to Anjali. Even Baba looked bored. There were several committees within the meeting, and each one was doing something small to help Gandhiji's movement. One woman had become a member of the All India

Women's Conference to help women in need, showing them how to spin on the charkha to earn a living and helping them learn to read. Two young men were planning a protest against imported clothes. A doctor was treating Dalit families in a neighboring village free of charge. An old man was running a small printing press to spread word of the freedom fight.

It all sounded so small when Anjali listened to the freedom fighters talk about what they were doing. How could it help free India of their foreign rulers, especially with their own leader, Gandhiji, still stuck in jail? He'd been there for months now with no release date in sight.

But her mother trusted in the freedom fight. She said this was how freedom would be won, with everyone doing their tiny part to fix what they could and make all Indians equal so that they could stand even stronger in peaceful protest against the Brits. And even if her mother's school integration didn't cause the British to leave, it was helping Paro and the other Dalit children. Someone was benefiting. Someone's life was improving. Wasn't that good enough?

When the meeting was finished, Anjali followed her parents down the circular stairway, being careful not to step on the backs of anyone's feet. Her mother was deep in discussion with Keshavji and the doctor as they made their way past the beautiful saris on display and out the store door. While Baba hung back with Balkishan, talking about politics, Anjali followed Ma outside.

The narrow alley brought with it a smoky smell, courtesy of a house down the street making kebabs. Anjali scrunched her nose at the smell of seared mutton, feeling sad for whatever goat or lamb was killed to make the meal.

"Ma," she said, squeezing between Keshavji and the doctor to tug at her mother's sari, "let's go home."

"Yes, Anjali, as soon as we finish planning—"

"Mrs. Joshi?" a tall man in a khaki uniform asked.

Six Indian policemen moved to surround them.

"Yes, that's me. Is there a problem?" asked Anjali's mother.

Anjali hid behind her, clinging tightly to the rough cotton of Ma's sari. She didn't like the way the officers smelled, like tobacco and tandoori chicken, and she eyed their lathis with fear.

"We have orders to arrest you, Mrs. Joshi."

"Arrest me?"

"For instigating riots with your Untouchables."

"These are exactly the kind of trumped-up charges we were worried about," the doctor said, his voice starting to rise.

But Keshavji put a calming hand on the doctor's forearm before turning to the police. "The riots are communal. Muslims and Hindus fighting each other. It is totally unrelated to her work with the Dalit community. This must be a mistake."

One policeman sneered at Keshavji, eyeing his scar. "Trying to be a hero or something?"

Anjali dug her fingers into her mother's waist, not wanting to let her go. How could the Indian policemen harass their fellow Indians, the very people who were trying to free India?

"Who are you?" the officer continued. "Why do you care?"

"I'm Keshav Parmar—"

Suddenly three policemen surrounded Keshavji.

"It's my lucky day." The officer smirked. "You're wanted for arrest too. For disturbing the peace with the protests you've planned and encouraging violent riots. Thanks for showing up at the same place and saving me some time."

Anjali's mother and Keshavji were handcuffed.

"No!" cried Anjali, desperately pawing at a policeman. "Let her go. Let my mother go!"

The doctor tried to pull Anjali back when the officer raised his lathi.

"Anjali!" shouted her mother.

"Back! Get back, or we'll throw you in jail too," shouted the officer, giving Anjali a push.

Anjali fell to the ground hard. Dirt coated her ghagra-choli, and her wrist was skinned.

"Go tell your father what has happened," Ma blurted as she was being pulled away. "Don't worry about us. We'll be fine. I'll be fine. Jai Hind!"

Still on the ground, Anjali reached for Ma's comforting hand, but her mother was hauled into the police van too quickly. "Ma!"

Someone grabbed Anjali's arm and pulled her off the ground, away from her mother, through the small crowd.

"Let go of me! Let me go!" She wrestled with the oily hand holding onto her elbow, but it was no use. "I said let me go!"

The smell of betel leaf filled her nostrils, and Anjali froze. She looked up. "Masterji?"

"Hurry, Anjali," said her teacher, pulling her arm again. "We must get you to your father. Fast. They're after me too."

Confused, Anjali followed her teacher as he pushed his way through the small cluster of bystanders, avoiding eye contact with the officers in the police van, and got to her father, who was exiting the shop still in enthusiastic discussion with Balkishan.

"Ma's been arrested!" Anjali shouted.

Baba's face dropped. "I have to help her. Can you—"

Masterji nodded. "I'll get her home." As Baba rushed away, Masterji ran with Anjali in the other direction, through the winding lanes, past crowded tenements, past the river and its fishy stench, until they could not run anymore.

They came to a stop outside the Regal Hotel, a one-story building with the smell of English pastries wafting out its arched doorway. Masterji hailed a rickshaw.

"Past Pragati, right at the street before the Marble Mosque. Madhuban Colony," directed Masterji. He turned to Anjali. "Don't worry, Anjali. Everything will be okay."

CHAPTER 23

*I*t turned out nothing was okay. Baba had tried to get Ma released and failed. She had been moved from the holding cell to prison, where she had been sitting for three days with no way out.

Three long, awful, scary days. And without school or Irfaan to distract her, Anjali missed Ma almost every second of the day.

She missed her in the morning, when Jamuna put coconut oil in Anjali's hair instead of Ma. She missed her whenever she saw the idol of Krishna sitting in their home temple with no one to perform his bath. And she missed her anytime she saw the rickety charkha lying in the hall, gathering dust.

Anjali picked up a wad of raw cotton and spun

wobbly wheel fast, so fast that her fingers burned. But no matter how hard she spun, she couldn't get the cotton to string out into a strand. Her mother always got it started for her when they would spin cotton for their clothes. Anjali felt the throbbing of tears in her eyes, and before she knew what she was doing, she shoved the spinning wheel across the floor.

It slammed into the wall, denting the already-weak wood of the old charkha.

Anjali's father rushed into the hall.

"It hurts." Anjali's voice quivered as she squeezed her right hand.

Her father knelt by her side. "I miss her too," he said gently.

"You keep telling me everything will be okay. But I don't think you're right. I feel sick every time I hear the news. The riots outside. Did you know an old man was killed when the Muslims and Hindus fought each other? In Ratnapur Society. Just a fifteen-minute walk from here. Maybe . . . maybe Ma is safest in jail. The rioters can't hurt her there."

"No," her father said. "Your mother belongs with us, Anjali. And I'm going to see to it that we get her out of that prison."

Anjali just stared at the damaged charkha, lying on its side, wheel spinning aimlessly.

Her father sighed. He went to the wooden cupboards built into the walls in their main hall and began sifting through some papers.

"Something for the lawyers?" Anjali asked.

Baba shook his head. "Here it is." He pulled out a wrinkled piece of paper with a crayon drawing of a crowned woman on a horse, holding a sword high. "Remember this?" he asked Anjali, handing her the drawing.

Anjali ran her fingers over the thin paper and the waxy bumps from her crayon marks. "My Rani of Jhansi drawing."

"You made it for Ma years ago. With the crayons Irfaan gave you that Diwali."

"She kept it?" Anjali asked.

"Of course she did. Even though the horse looks more like a cat."

Anjali couldn't help but smile.

"She kept it, Anju, because it is the Rani of Jhansi. Because you used to ask for that story every night for bedtime for an entire year when you were little. Do you remember the story?"

Anjali shrugged. "We learned about her in school

too. She was a brave queen who led her subjects in battle against the British almost a hundred years ago." She paused. "But why did Ma tell me that story if she believes in ahimsa? It's full of war and weapons."

Her father sat down next to her. "It was a different time. No one could ever think back then that independence could be won through nonviolence. They just knew of no other weapons other than physical ones." Baba patted Anjali's head. "Do you remember why you would ask for that story every night?"

Anjali shook her head. She barely remembered hearing that bedtime story as a child.

"You used to think it was a story about Ma."

Anjali nodded. "I do sort of remember that. Because she was so strong. And I was four."

"That's right. Now, why don't we go for a short walk? It's early, and the rioters have been out all night. They must be asleep."

"But that old man just died in Ratnapur Society."

"That was at night. It's daylight. And we're not going in that direction. Besides, we'll turn back at the first sign of danger. So who should we go see? Irfaan?"

Anjali shook her head. "He doesn't want to see me."

"Well, you have an entire basti of friends just a few

minutes away. I think they're due a visit, don't you?"

Although she the throbbing pain in her heart from her mother's absence was still strong, Anjali couldn't help but smile.

Anjali had wrapped herself in her grandmother's wool shawl, preparing herself for the cool morning air and anything else they would face. But the five-minute walk to the basti was totally uneventful. There wasn't a person on the street. No peacocks to be seen, either— just a lone stray cat slinking in the shadows. It felt disconcerting and totally unlike their town, but at least Anjali knew that with no other humans in sight, she and her father would be safe. She also knew Ma would be happy Anjali and her father had gone to check on their friends at a time like this.

Other than a little smoke damage in the back alley, the homes seemed to have been untouched by the riots. While Anjali's father spoke to the basti elders and gave them the children's tiffin containers, Anjali spotted Mohan sitting under a tree, stringing some metal trinkets and seeds into a necklace.

"It's beautiful," she said.

Mohan shrugged. "I started it last evening. Just something to do while we're stuck inside like prisoners thanks to the riots."

Anjali looked down.

"I . . . I shouldn't have said that," Mohan stammered. "I'm sorry. I heard about your mother."

Anjali nodded. She was determined not to cry here. Ma would want her to be strong and brave, like she always was.

"My own mother died when I was ten," said Mohan, putting the last few round seeds on the necklace. "It was just a small fever. But it started spiking. We needed medicine to get the fever down. But no doctor would see us. And when someone finally told us the name of the medicine that would bring the fever down, we couldn't afford it. We could barely afford to eat, you know." He tied the two ends of the string together, completing the necklace. "Within a couple hours, she was gone, and I was left with no one."

Anjali felt awful. Mohan was telling the story so nonchalantly. Like he was so used to pain and horrible things happening to him, it was just to be expected.

"She is the one who taught me how to make these necklaces," Mohan added softly.

"Then she lives on in every one of them," said Anjali.

Mohan gently put his necklace down.

"I was afraid you would have gotten stuck at the fair during the riots when you were selling your necklaces," Anjali added.

Mohan shook his head. "I didn't go. Didn't want to cause trouble."

"I'm so sorry about school being closed. And I'm even more sorry about being forced to sit in the back. It's just not right. I don't know how you can take all these injustices." Anjali cleared her throat. "I meant it when I said your necklaces were beautiful. So let's go show the world your art. Let's set up shop right outside the basti."

Mohan looked at Anjali, speechless.

"Right outside on the street. Just for a few minutes to see if we get any customers."

"This is how it works in your world, huh? You have an idea, and people everywhere make way for it to come true?"

"Come on. It's just something to do," Anjali added, giving Mohan a nudge with her hand.

Mohan couldn't help but smile.

Anjali and Mohan stood right outside the basti on the footpath, around the corner from Captain Brent's bungalow, ready to rush back inside at the first sign of danger. They were each holding a handful of Mohan's necklaces. But with no one on the street, there were no customers, either.

"Maybe this was a bad idea," said Mohan.

"It's a great idea. But it might be bad timing," said Anjali, smiling at a lone tan puppy with crooked ears who hesitantly crawled out from behind a pile of trash.

Mohan shook his head. "You're very optimistic," he said.

Anjali shrugged, crouching to pet the dog. "I have faith."

"You remind me of a horse."

Anjali paused. "A horse?"

"That white horse with the pink feathers tied to its head. The one that you kids pay to ride." Anjali shook her head. "I don't do that. I feel bad for that poor horse."

Mohan smiled gently. "Of course you do." He paused. "What I mean is, that horse has those gold-and-pink blinders next to his eyes so he doesn't see anything else around him. Doesn't get panicked. You have blinders on. We walk the same path, but our experiences are so different."

Mohan pointed at the orange triangular flags flying from a temple a few streets over. "That temple you freely enter? That's where I was once screamed at by an old lady because I tripped on the street in front of the temple and accidentally grazed a woman who had just bathed for her prayers."

His eyes welled up at the memory.

"That paanwalla's shop you get your treats from? That's where a group of rich kids from your street once threw stones at me because I dared to look in their direction. They said I was casting the evil eye on them. And I could do nothing back, even though I was twice their size."

Anjali's chest tightened. Even the smiling, panting little puppy in front of her couldn't make her feel better.

"And that dog you're petting . . . that dog has more freedom to go places in this town than I do. Because some people don't mind if a dog's tongue licks them. But they are bothered to their core if my shadow falls on them."

Now Anjali's eyes were the ones filling with tears.

She blinked them back. "I'm sorry. This is a bad idea. I was wrong," she said, getting up and sending the puppy on its way.

"Wait. Maybe your optimism isn't always a bad thing," Mohan said, staring into the distance.

Anjali followed his gaze. A car sped around the corner and parked in front of Captain Brent's office. An armed British officer and his wife got out, escorted by a couple police officers. The officer kept looking around the deserted streets nervously, a hand near his holster. But his wife kept staring at Mohan and Anjali. She motioned to her husband that she would be back in a minute and crossed the street, two now-concerned police officers behind her. "What are you selling, young man?" she asked Mohan in broken Hindi.

"Bahut purane mani hain," answered Anjali, putting on a smile. "Antiques. They are all the rage. This one would look lovely against your beautiful dress." She held up a necklace of wooden beads as the larger of the two policemen opened his mouth to say something.

"It's lovely. I'll take it," the woman said, before the policeman had a chance. She ran a finger over the beaded necklace, her polished red nail glistening. "How much?"

"Whatever you see fit," replied Anjali.

The woman reached into her purse and gave Mohan a handful of coins. She put the necklace over her head and rushed back to her husband, who was waiting impatiently outside Captain Brent's gate. The policemen squinted hard at both children, giving them the *I'll be watching you* look, but didn't say anything as they followed the woman back.

Mohan turned to Anjali. "Purane mani?"

"Well, I didn't want to say they were broken pieces of wood you found on the side of the street," said Anjali, giggling with Mohan. "See? They don't care about the caste system one bit. And if they don't, why should Indians? Change is possible. Progress is possible. It may take time. But it is possible, isn't it?"

Mohan looked at Anjali. "You're a lot alike."

"Who?"

"Your mother may not be able to participate in the movement while she is imprisoned, but her work is living on in you."

CHAPTER 24

It took another day for the British Raj to give Anjali's father permission for them to visit her mother in jail.

Now as they entered the small prison, Anjali trembled at the thought of her mother's condition inside the jail. Would she be bruised from police beatings? Would she be hungry? Was she as scared as Anjali was?

Anjali's father put a reassuring hand on her back as he guided her through the stony corridors of the prison, holding the crayon drawing of the Rani of Jhansi. He had told Anjali her mother would be delighted to see that reminder of their past in her depressing cell.

The building was dark and dreary. The hallways

were bumpy and uneven. The walls were speckled with slimy black sludge, and the air stank like raw sewage. Although it wasn't as foul as the spinach farm, Anjali still had to hold her breath, taking in oxygen through her mouth only when necessary, to avoid inhaling the stench. Led by a short guard whose hair had been thoroughly greased with stinky mustard seed oil, they passed a cell so overcrowded, the male prisoners were practically lined limb to sweaty limb. The next cell over was just as packed with noisy prisoners. One mustached man was banging his head repeatedly on the bars. Anjali shivered, hurrying forward. The next cell over had just five prisoners.

They were the political prisoners.

Suddenly Anjali caught a glimpse of a familiar face. "Keshavji!" she exclaimed.

"Keep moving," the guard muttered, but Anjali paused anyway, hoping disobeying the guard wouldn't ruin her chances of seeing Ma.

Keshavji, still just as poised and inspiring as ever, was consoling a bearded prisoner. His eyes lit up. "Anjali! How is your mother, beta?" he asked, stepping over to the bars.

"We're about to see her," Anjali replied.

"She'll be fine. We all will be. Just you watch," Keshavji said.

Behind him, the bearded man began to cry silently into his palms. Keshavji glanced at the man and whispered to Anjali. "He's scheduled to hang in the spring."

Anjali stepped back. It was Mrs. Mishra's son. His mustache from the picture his mother carried with her was now a full beard from months of sitting in prison. His hazel eyes had dark circles under them. His clothes looked damp and filthy.

Before she could stare at him any longer, the guard tapped her shoulder. "I said move."

"Jai Hind!" Keshavji called after her. "Freedom will soon be ours!"

Baba put his arm around Anjali and ushered her forward, exiting out of the darkness and crossing a courtyard with patches of grass. The sun's rays made Anjali hopeful that her mother would be in as good spirits as Keshavji, but despite the warmth, Anjali couldn't help but shiver when they entered the women's prison. It was as dark and smelly as the men's. There, in the cell political prisoners were kept in, Anjali's mother stood next to a couple other women, her sandals touching the muck of the jail floor.

Anjali rushed to the bars. "Ma!"

Her parents fought back tears as Baba reached his hand through the cell to Ma's. "Shailaja," he said.

A lump rose in Anjali's throat. She had only seen her father cry once before, years back, when a letter from Chachaji had arrived telling him Anjali's grandmother had died in Bombay.

"Anju, why did you come?" Ma asked. "You must be scared."

"There are no windows here. Do you ever get to see the sun?" asked Anjali.

Ma forced a smile. "You're my sun. I'm seeing you now."

Anjali shook her head. "I mean it. What do you eat?"

"Cold daal and rice. Makes me miss Jamuna's cooking."

"And the bathroom. Where is the bathroom?"

Her mother's face flushed, and Anjali immediately felt bad for making Ma feel bad. What a foolish question of her to ask. There was no bathroom. That's why it smelled so awful in the prison. There was a pit toilet. The prisoners were forced to go in the pit toilet in the corners of their cells, a pit that was not cleaned out nearly as often as their latrine was at home. The evidence of that was tracked all over the cell, just like every other cell in the prison.

Anjali turned to her father. "We have to get her out, Baba."

He nodded. "We're talking to the lawyers, Shailaja. They're doing the best they can." He lowered his voice to a whisper so the guard couldn't hear. "Masterji and some others had to flee. They've gone north to Indore."

Her mother looked sad.

"But I saw Keshavji," Anjali said, "and he said, 'Freedom will soon be ours.'"

Ma's eyes shone with tears. Anjali felt like a snake was coiling around her stomach. *Why did I mention "freedom" when Ma is stuck in this jail?*

She changed the subject. "Mrs. Mishra's son was there too."

Ma nodded. "I knew he was being housed here. Poor child." She leaned into the bars, closer to Anjali. "You wanted to know why I quit working for Captain Brent suddenly, right?" She sighed. "Well, for several months, Anju, I was not doing the right thing. So many freedom fighters were being imprisoned as the Raj started to crack down on their activities. And so many parents and wives and husbands were coming to the Captain, asking him to pardon their family members. But he never said yes. Not once.

"Mrs. Mishra's son was the last straw. He was absolutely wrong to set fire to a building. And he is so lucky no one was in the building so no one got hurt. But no one got hurt, right? So he should serve his prison term and then be released. Instead, that seventeen-year-old boy is going to be hanged and lose his life. The punishment just doesn't fit the crime. They don't value Indian lives.

"That's when I realized the freedom movement needed all the help it could get if the British were just going to kill or imprison anyone who tried to stand up to them. And that's why I quit." Tears trickled down Ma's face. "But sometimes, Anju, when I am sitting here in a cell of my own waste . . . alone, cold, scared . . . I wonder . . . why did I quit?"

Anjali tried not to cry, but she couldn't stop the tears. Seeing her strong, brave mother reduced to this made her sad and scared, but also angry. They could not break her mother's spirit. And they could not stop the independence movement her mother and so many others had fought so hard for.

Anjali reached for her childhood drawing in her

father's hand and passed it through the bars. But her mother only cried harder upon seeing it.

"I wasn't wrong, you know," Anjali said softly.

Ma wiped away her tears.

"All those years ago . . ." Anjali steadied her voice. "You are as brave and as strong as the Rani of Jhansi." She squeezed her mother's hand. "You did the right thing, Ma. And the British will not win. You will not remain in prison. We promise."

CHAPTER 25

*A*njali's mother had been stuck behind bars for nine days now. It was strange to think Ma had been out of their house for so long. Baba saw the lawyers every couple days to see if there was an update, but the news was always the same: no news. There were still violent clashes between Hindus and Muslims every so often on the other side of town and in the business district, so school continued to be closed. Plus, with Masterji still hiding in Indore, they didn't know who would take over running the school for him.

That afternoon, Baba had taken a long time to return from the lawyers. Anjali hoped the rioters weren't at it again, and that her father was safe. She paced on the porch, scratching away at some mosquito bites on her fingers, looking over the blooming plumeria tree in the front yard for any sign of her father, and finally breathed easier as she saw him open their gate.

"You took so long!" she exclaimed as she rushed to his side, ignoring the bites that were now pinker and puffier than before, thanks to all her scratching. "Is there good news? Will Ma be let out?"

"Not yet. But the lawyers sound hopeful that maybe she will get out of prison before poor Gandhiji. You know he's still fasting?"

Anjali shook her head. She had stopped listening to the radio in the mornings because the news of the previous night's violence was always too upsetting.

"Come. Let's listen to something inspirational on the radio for once."

Anjali sat with her father near the radio as Chachaji napped in his room and Jamuna cooked their dinner. Although Keshavji was still in jail, a new announcer was telling the story of how Gandhi decided to start a twenty-one-day fast in February to protest against the British inciting Hindu-Muslim violence to derail the freedom movement. He was only taking the juice of citrus fruits mixed with water as he remained imprisoned by the British behind unnecessary barbed wire in the city of Poona.

Twenty-one days. Anjali was stunned. She felt hungry after just a few hours. And he had been in jail since last August. More than five months. Yet he was still making a difference. And still as strong and stubborn as ever.

"What a man," said Baba, his eyes filled with awe. He put his arm around Anjali. "What a person, I should have said. Your mother is strong and making a difference too, Anju. I'm so proud of her—and you," he added tearfully. "I have a new list. My mother, your mother, and now you."

"A list of what?" Anjali asked.

"The bravest people I know."

An angry shout from outside interrupted him.

Anjali felt her heartbeat quicken. Were rioters right outside their house again?

She and her father rushed outside for a better look. Lakshmi Auntie and her husband, Sharad Uncle, were on the side of the street with Suman and a bunch of other men. They were huddled around something, kicking and shouting furiously.

Anjali's father hurried to open the gate, and they rushed to the mob. "What's going on?" asked Baba.

Lakshmi Auntie's face was a deep red. "This . . . this filthy animal dared to give a disgusting toilet necklace to my daughter! Thank God my husband noticed this piece of garbage before he got any closer to Suman. She would have been ruined. No one would have married my beautiful daughter!"

Anjali's stomach sank. "Mohan," she said desperately, begging her father to do something.

Baba pulled the mob away from Mohan. He lay crumpled on the ground, his shirt soaked in blood.

The crowd gasped as Baba grabbed Mohan.

"He's touching him!" their neighbor Vivek shouted. Another neighbor, Ashwin Uncle, who was always so kind to Anjali, giving her guavas off their tree whenever they were ripe, had Mohan's blood splattered on his sandal and toes.

"You touched him too when you kicked him!" shouted Anjali. But then Baba got Mohan to his feet, and Anjali almost lost her lunch when she saw her friend's face. Teeth were missing. One eye socket looked smashed in. There was blood everywhere. Then Anjali saw the seashell necklace in Mohan's clenched fist—the same necklace Leela Chitnis had on in the newspaper. He must have decided to give it to Suman because he thought she looked like the famous movie star. Even worse, Anjali thought, he must have tried to give it to Suman because Anjali had told him his jewelry was so beautiful no one would care who made it. This was all her fault.

"Let me go," Mohan mumbled to Anjali's father.

"But—"

"Please . . ."

Anjali's father let go, and Mohan hobbled down the road.

Even Suman looked a little ill from all the violence done to Mohan. Her hands were trembling so much, her bangles shivered on her wrist. Anjali's fury built. She took a step in Mohan's direction when Sharad Uncle started shouting at Baba.

"Oh, you're so brave now, Professor!" Sharad Uncle bellowed. "But we all know you let your wife put herself in danger while you hide behind your college job!"

Baba stood his ground. "We aren't backward like you. My wife is a strong woman who can do anything. And so is my daughter. You will not intimidate us anymore— Anjali!"

Baba's words cut off as Anjali chased after Mohan. She couldn't just leave him to die.

"Mohan, wait!" Anjali yelled as she caught up to him. "We need to get you help."

Mohan looked at Anjali with bloodied eyes now uneven from the beating. "You've done enough."

"Please. I don't want what happened to your mother to happen to you. There's a doctor. I remember him speaking at the freedom fighters' meeting. He treats Dalits."

"Untouchables," said Mohan.

"No."

"Call us what we are. What we always will be. You think you're changing the world, Anjali? You're not making any difference. Letting a few Untouchables sit in the back of your classroom will not stop another Untouchable mother from dying of a simple fever. It won't stop us from being burned for daring to have a drink of water on a hot day. And it won't stop a kid from being killed for giving someone a present."

"But you're hurt. You need help!" Anjali pleaded, her voice cracking.

"I said, you've done enough. I'm leaving town. You

can't help me. Accept it. And accept that nothing will ever change."

All Anjali could do was watch as Mohan limped away, disappearing over the hilly road and leaving nothing but a few bloody footprints in the dirt.

CHAPTER 26

Shortly after Mohan left town, Gandhiji's fast finally came to an end on March fourth. Tensions were easing between Hindus and Muslims. The newspaper was once again regularly delivered. Baba's college reopened, and word was that Anjali's school would open at the end of the month with a new teacher, right after Holi, the festival of colors. And best of all, Anjali and her father were finally able to visit her mother again.

Taking a break from worrying if Paro and the other children from the basti would be hurt like Mohan if they sat in the back of the classroom—or if they would even be allowed in school at all, depending on who the new teacher was, after what Suman's family did to Mohan—Anjali tried to focus on Ma instead as she entered the prison with Baba. She ran past the male prisoners, stopping only briefly to say hello to Keshavji. He gave Anjali a thundering "Jai Hind!" as she rushed out through the courtyard toward the women's prison.

There the other prisoners were sitting cross-legged on the mucky floor, eating their daal and rice, but Anjali's mother was standing in a corner.

"Ma, we're here," said Anjali breathlessly into the shadowy cell.

"Anjali?" Ma said weakly, turning to them, her once-clean sari now a dingy brown. "Are you excited for Holi, Anju? You have to promise to become a colorful mess for me—"

"Your face—" Anjali gasped when her mother got closer. Ma's cheeks were deflated, deprived of their rosy hue. Her eyes looked glassy, like tears were permanently ready to fall. Anjali couldn't stand the sight of her mother looking so sick. How much longer would she be stuck in this tiny cell? It seemed unnatural, like that poor pacing lioness at the zoo in Bombay Chachaji had once taken her to.

Ma stood as straight as she could as she neared

them. "You know, I thought a lot about what you said, Anju. And you were right. We must continue the fight. We cannot let them scare us into quitting."

"We will never give up the fight, Shailaja," said Baba, reaching for her hand. "But you must not give up on yourself, either. What has happened to you? Are they feeding you all right?"

Ma held on to the prison bars like they were the only thing keeping her up. "I'm fasting. Like Gandhiji. The whole prison has been talking about his fast. I'm only taking lime juice with some water." She pointed to a small steel vessel behind her.

Anjali was stunned. "You're fasting? But you're not Gandhiji! No one is going to care if you stop eating. Besides, his fast is over. Didn't you hear? Please. You have to eat—for me. I need you. Tell her, Baba."

"That's why I'm doing this, Anju," said Ma. "So that my child can grow up in a free country."

Anjali shook her head. None of this made sense. Her mother didn't have the clout that Gandhiji had. No newspaper was going to cover this fast. And the British would probably be happy if Anjali's mom starved to death. One less freedom fighter to worry about. Besides, who said fasting was the answer? Gandhiji had been wrong before. He was wrong to call Dalits "Harijans." He was wrong to burn clothes. She had to snap her mother out of this. "Mohan left."

"Anjali," said Baba, shaking his head at her.

"No. Ma should know. Sharad Uncle and our neighbors beat him up badly. He was so hurt, Ma. He left town. He's not going to join my school." She paused. "He might be dead."

Ma's face fell. "Anju, I'm so sorry."

"Mohan's gone. Irfaan's gone. My two closest friends are gone. The school is closed and Masterji is also gone. It felt like everybody was just quitting. And if they could quit, why couldn't I? Why shouldn't I? I don't ever again want someone to look at me the way Mohan did that day. Besides, this fight seems impossible. How can we change the course of history? Is it even possible to stop the British? We couldn't even stop our neighbors from hurting Mohan. It all seemed pointless. But now that I see you here . . . I'm not going to quit. I'm not going to give up. I'm going to keep fighting for what you started. One way or another, I'm going to continue your work. Paro and her friends will go to school because that's what's right."

Anjali's mother beamed at her proudly.

"But you can't quit, either."

Ma shook her head. "I won't. You know how stubborn I can be." She smiled at Anjali's father, but he didn't return the smile. "Don't think a little lack of food will get me down."

"I'm not saying don't quit your fast. I mean don't quit on *me*."

"Time's up," mumbled the guard from behind.

Palms suddenly clammy, Anjali spoke as fast as she could. "If your fast doesn't work—if it doesn't get you out of jail, you can't quit on life. Just eat that horrible cold daal they give you and get your energy up so that we can see you back at home soon. Promise?"

"I said, time's up," said the guard, his hand on Anjali's shoulder and Baba's back, nudging them away.

Anjali turned back. "Promise, Ma?"

Her mother shakily whispered, "Jai Hind."

She didn't promise. Anjali's took one last look at her frail mother before the guard ushered her and her father out.

CHAPTER 27

"Three hundred and seven," Anjali said, writing the number with a stick in the dirt in front of her house. That was how many hours she had calculated her mother had been fasting over the past week and a half.

The graffiti on their compound wall grew with each night too. The words *caste polluters*, *Untouchable*, and *filth* were scrawled all across their concrete wall. Anjali felt even worse about painting the Q on Captain Brent's wall now.

On the porch behind her, Chachaji sipped noisily at his tea. It was often hard to tell on his face, which seemed to permanently have a scowl etched into it, but Anjali could have sworn she saw new wrinkles near his eyes. Wrinkles of worry for Anjali's mother. A part of Anjali wanted to hug the old man, to ask him to play cards with her like they used to when he had first moved in with them. But a part of her could not forgive him for the way he'd acted with Mohan.

Anjali couldn't sit around waiting any longer for her father to return with news from his meeting with the attorneys. She had made a promise to her mother, and she had to keep it. School was set to open the day after Holi. She had to go see it and make sure everything was ready. Anjali didn't even know who would be in charge, with Masterji in hiding in Indore. Would the new teacher still agree to integrate the school the way Masterji had? That was a new level of worry Anjali wasn't sure she could tackle yet.

Anjali told Chachaji to let Baba know where she was going and headed out of her compound. The vegetable vendor was once again pushing his cart in the streets, but there were still fewer people out and about than normal. She rounded the corner, heading for school. There was just one kid in line at the street's paanwalla's shop in the distance. Anjali squinted in the sun as she got closer. The boy had curly hair, but it took a moment for her to recognize him.

"Irfaan?" she blurted.

Irfaan turned, holding his paan. His father was standing nearby and waved to Anjali.

Anjali started to wave back to Farhan Uncle but paused. Irfaan was glaring at her, looking at her with eyes that had turned to stone. She could barely recognize her friend. Irfaan grabbed his father's hand and pulled him away.

Anjali just watched as they rounded the corner and Irfaan disappeared from her sight.

It's for the best, she thought, trying hard to convince herself. She passed the paanwalla, headed up the hill to school, passed the peepal tree, and froze. The little wooden arch above the entrance with the name *Pragati* painted on it was broken. And the splintered wooden door underneath it was hanging by one hinge.

Anjali squeezed through the opening, trying to step around the debris, but it was everywhere. Her classroom had been ransacked. The wooden benches were broken into pieces. The tables had legs broken off. The chalkboard looked like someone had pummeled it with a hammer.

Anjali backed away, out of the building, running smack into something.

She gasped, scared it was a rioter. But it was her father with a stack of papers from the courthouse.

"Baba!" she cried, throwing her arms around him. "They've destroyed everything. Now how will school open after Holi? How will Paro ever go to school?"

"We'll fix it."

"How? Everything is going wrong. Irfaan left me. Ma is in jail. Mohan is not even trying to fight for what's right."

"I heard you saying something like that to Ma the other day." Baba smoothed Anjali's hair out of her face. "About Mohan. But that's not really a true statement, Anjali."

Anjali wiped at her tears. "What do you mean?"

"He isn't giving up on you. He isn't quitting because the going got tough. It has *always* been tough for Mohan. Look what these people have done to the school," Baba said as he moved pieces of the broken arch to one corner. "Imagine what they could do to him. And despite that, he risked everything to join you at school, to support your idea. You just saw a *taste* of what life can be like for Mohan when the neighbors attacked him. Who knows what they would have done if no one stopped them?"

"So you're saying he was right to leave?" Anjali asked, adding two more pieces of broken wood to the pile Baba was making.

Baba shrugged. "I'm saying that is not for us to judge. Only he knows what is right and wrong for him."

"And Irfaan? He thinks I painted those horrible things about Muslims on his dairy. He's blaming me for what other Hindus did!"

"Did you blame him for what other Muslims did?" Baba asked.

Anjali fiddled with her right braid, not wanting to answer.

Baba took the bottom of her other braid and fanned it in her face, tickling her nose to try to get a response. But Anjali kept her mouth shut, not wanting to admit Baba was right.

"It's okay if you did. As long as you now realize it was wrong. Irfaan just needs time too. Everyone does. Like Ma once said."

"No. Enough time. I'm sick of having to wait. How much longer until Ma comes home?"

Baba squeezed Anjali's hand. "I'm so sorry, beta. I wish I had some good news for you."

"What did the new lawyer say?" she asked.

Anjali's father shook his head.

"What is it, Baba?"

He sighed. "I'm sorry, Anju. I tried. I even gave him some of our savings to see if it could change things."

"A bribe?" asked Anjali, shocked. Bribing officials was not uncommon in India. It was how a lot of people got their daily tasks done, like getting admitted into a hospital faster or getting a building permit approved. But Anjali's parents had always frowned upon the practice.

"But that's against the Gandhian way," she said. "You always said corruption will be the death of a free India."

Her father looked down, his hands quivering. "I was desperate."

Anjali immediately felt awful for making her father feel so bad. "It doesn't matter. It's okay, Baba."

"The lawyer says the British will not budge on her imprisonment. They're using the riots as an excuse to get as many of the freedom fighters as they can off the streets. They need things to calm down so they can maintain their control. And now that Gandhiji's fast is over, and the riots are less common, I don't think anything will change for her."

Anjali shook her head. This was not okay. Three

hundred and seven hours might not have been a lot of time to some people. But without food, it was a *long* time. She had to get her mother out before she died behind bars. There was just one way.

Anjali was going to have to ask Captain Brent for help.

Again.

CHAPTER 28

*W*ith her father by her side, Anjali walked down the dusty street toward the captain's office. "I'm sure he'll listen to us. Especially after everything that has happened."

They passed the basti. Anjali kept walking. She was too scared to see Paro and her grandmother after what happened to Mohan. Too scared they would hate her.

There was still an hour to go until nightfall, but people had been so accustomed to the curfew that now no one was out in the streets, even though it had been lifted for the big Holi celebrations tomorrow.

There was just one figure crouching on the footpath, a couple houses from Captain Brent's bungalow, in a faded old sari stained with tears. It was Mrs. Mishra. She was hugging the tattered picture of her son and sobbing. Anjali's stomach dropped.

Holi is the festival of spring, Anjali thought as she remembered Mrs. Mishra begging for her son's life to be spared before he was to be hanged in the spring. They must have just executed the boy for his crime. Anjali felt a little guilty for not bothering to look for him when she visited the prison the last time.

Anjali looked sadly at her father. She tried to come up with something to say to the old woman. She wanted to tell her that she had seen him in jail last month. She wanted to tell Mrs. Mishra how very sorry she was.

Baba nodded at Anjali. He cleared his throat, and Mrs. Mishra looked up. "We are so sorry for your loss, Mrs. Mishra," said Baba.

Mrs. Mishra wiped the tears off her son's picture. But the more she tried to clean it, the more she just ended up smearing it with her fingerprints. "You're *sorry?*"

Baba nodded.

Mrs. Mishra sneered. "If your wife had spent a little less time with those people and a little more time worrying about her own kind, he could have been saved," she said softly, as another tear plopped onto the picture she had just tried to clean.

Anajli couldn't believe that this woman, angrily scrubbing away at a picture, was the same person who meekly begged Captain Brent to help her last year. But she told herself that Mrs. Mishra had just lost her son and wasn't thinking straight. Besides, Baba would know exactly what to say to calm her down.

"*Those* people?" whispered Baba, his voice shaking.

Anjali could feel her pulse nervously beating in her neck as Baba continued. "We are terribly sorry for your loss, Mrs. Mishra," he said. "But I won't have you badmouthing my wife or blaming her for something that was out of her hands. Those people, as you call them, are no different than you or I, and don't you forget it."

Anjali squeezed her father's hand. "Baba, please!" After a moment, he followed her away.

He straightened out his khadi kurta as they neared the gate to Captain Brent's bungalow. "I'm sorry. With your mother still stuck in jail . . . I don't know what got into me. I should go back and apologize to her—"

But Anjali pulled on her father's arm, eager to get

to their destination. All this talk with Mrs. Mishra had her worried. Would they hang her mother too? She hadn't destroyed any British property. Maybe she'd be safe. Or maybe they would blame the damage the rioters caused on her. Either way, Anjali had to hurry to talk to Captain Brent. Before it was too late.

At Captain Brent's office, several armed policemen now stood around the gate that was once, just months earlier, so easily to vandalize. She tried to calm her nerves to walk by them and their long rifles.

But one of the policemen stepped in front of her. "What is your business here?"

"We need to speak to Captain Brent," said Anjali's father.

The man's eyes narrowed.

"Please," Anjali chimed in. "I need to ask his help." She hated this admission. She hated that she had to be here. But maybe Brent Sahib had changed, like Baba had said, after everything that had happened. He had saved her life, after all. He had proven he had a heart. He wouldn't have saved her if he hadn't cared for her. He must have cared for Anjali's mother too.

Of course he does, thought Anjali. *She worked for him*

for an entire year. And she was a hard worker. Of course he cares for her.

The police officer eyed Anjali up and down and then motioned for her to pass. "Make it quick," he said gruffly.

Anjali turned to her father. "Baba, I can do this."

Baba shook his head. "You're a child. I'm not letting you go in there alone."

Anjali lowered her voice. "Trust me. You want me to be strong, right? To never go through what your mother went through?"

"But . . ."

Anjali looked her father right in the eyes. "Do you really believe that new list of yours? Or is it just something you said to be nice?"

Baba sighed, taking a seat on the porch steps. "I'm right here if you need me," he said, motioning for Anjali to enter the bungalow.

A new secretary took down Anjali's information and led her to the sitting room. Anjali briefly wondered what had happened to her mother's replacement. Had she too grown sick of Captain Brent's decrees and refusals to write pardons? Or worse, had something happened to her in the riots?

Captain Brent was on his silk sofa with a pen, hunched over a pile of papers. "Just look at this. A bus burned down in Hyderabad. Three British officers stabbed in Delhi. Hindu-Muslim riots in Calcutta. There's something bloody wrong with you people," he huffed to his secretary before catching sight of Anjali. "You," he said. "What are you doing here?"

"My mother's been arrested," said Anjali shakily.

Captain Brent nodded. "I was sorry to hear that."

Anjali breathed easier. She knew it. Captain Brent cared about her and her mother. He was going to help them. "They arrested her because she wanted to integrate Dalit children into my school."

"I see nothing wrong with that. You're all the same in my eyes," said Captain Brent, putting down the stack of papers.

Anjali brightened. "So you'll do it?"

"Do what?"

"You'll write a letter of pardon on behalf of the Raj so she can get out of prison?"

Captain Brent scoffed. "Tell me, what was she arrested for again?"

"For wanting to let Dalit children attend our school."

"Wrong," said Captain Brent, sifting through papers.

"Here it is. For inciting violence with her actions and fiery words. She was being irresponsible during a delicate time when everyone's sensitivities were raised. The riots grew worse."

"The riots were between Hindus and Muslims. Besides, Ma never made a fiery speech. She never protested. These charges are just an excuse to get a freedom fighter off the street."

Captain Brent squeezed the pen in his hand so tight his knuckles turned a ghostly white.

Anjali's voice softened. "She worked for you for a year. Don't you care about her?"

"I care about the law. About my duty."

She felt the sting of tears, but she forced them back. She was not going to cry in front of this man. "But you saved me—"

"I saved you from those thugs because that was my duty. Writing a pardon letter when a crime was committed is not. I won't support anyone who helps this land crumble into violence. Now get yourself home. It's almost dark. Have you seen your school? There's no longer a curfew, but you never know when you people will start rioting again."

The secretary started to lead Anjali out, but Anjali

stopped. "If they're still rioting while my mother is in jail, doesn't that prove her actions aren't inciting violence?"

The pen slipped out of Captain Brent's grasp, dropping noisily onto the slate floor as the secretary ushered her out.

CHAPTER 29

The streets were finally full of crowds again on Holi, as people celebrated the colors of spring by filling the world with colored powder made from dried vegetables, flowers, and herbs, and colored water sprayed through pichkaris. Children and adults alike pumped the handles of the long tubes, which spat out splashes of colored water everywhere.

Holi was the great equalizer. Everyone wore white, and by the time the day was done, they were so coated in pinks, blues, greens, and yellows that you couldn't tell anyone's caste or religion.

It was also a time for merriment. Everyone would dance and sing in their yards and on the street, throwing handfuls of color on strangers and family members with equal vigor. Townspeople would play pranks, trying to douse one another with color when they least suspected it.

Anjali used to race through the streets with her pichkari, Irfaan by her side, spraying boisterous kids dancing, old uncles playing drums, and aunties singing and laughing in circles. Unlike the other neighbors, Suman would dress in all white, but she wanted nothing to do with the messy rituals, and sulked in a corner the moment some grains of colored powder made it onto her clothes. Anjali and Irfaan always made it a point to spray her, declaring whoever got her first the winner.

Back then, Irfaan didn't mind the Hindu festival, Anjali thought as she watched her neighbors from her porch. Everyone was squealing with excitement as cold splashes of orange and pink came shooting out of pichkaris at them. Music carried from down the street, along with the sounds of more people.

Of course, back then, things were different.

This was normally a time of joy and celebration, but with her mother fasting in jail for days, Paro without a school to attend, Mohan no longer in town, and Irfaan no longer her friend, Anjali felt no joy and had nothing to celebrate. She hadn't even bothered wearing an old white outfit for the festivities. Everything seemed hopeless and dark, despite all the bursts of color floating in the air.

The lawyers had no answers for how to get Ma out of jail, and Anjali had no clue how to keep her promise to her mother and integrate the Dalit children into her school now that the school had been destroyed. How could she, when the only other student in her class who was willing to help was no longer talking to her? And how could she take this risk with Paro's life, with all her friends' lives, after the way Anjali's own neighbors had beaten Mohan almost to death—or maybe *to* death?

Anjali fought back tears from the cot on the porch. Her father stood in the garden, feeding the street dogs and stray cats that found their way into the compound. Finally, after all these days, the animals had returned. They must have been so scared with the riots, and with no one in the streets, it must have been hard for them to find food too. These wretched riots had made things bad for everyone. Anjali watched hungrily as her father threw a handful of rice out for the sparrows and parrots in their yard. But she had yet to spot a peacock.

Chachaji stepped out onto the porch and plugged his ears. "How much longer is this racket going to go on for? When I was a child, we never did this nonsense. And how much longer is your father going to feed those beasts before we can eat our dinner?" he grumbled.

Anjali didn't respond.

"We should find you a husband and get you married before they ruin your life too with this useless fight against the Raj," he muttered, then went back inside.

That did it. Anjali got up. She couldn't stand being at home. She rushed down the porch steps, past her father.

"Where are you going, Anju?" he asked. "Don't you want dinner?"

Anjali shook her head. "I'm not hungry."

She closed the iron gate behind her and walked down the street. This year's Holi looked exactly like last year's, as if the riots had never happened at all. All around her, excited kids were running, chucking handfuls of powder at one another and ducking from the onslaught of color. A group of drummers was drinking quick sips of thandai, milk mixed with water, sugar, and spices, in between banging their instruments to the crowd's delight.

But Holi just wasn't the same without her mother to sing songs and dance with.

Anjali scanned the road for peacock feathers, for anything that would make her feel happy on what used to be her favorite holiday, but there were no feathers, and without her mother, life as she knew it was forever altered. There was nothing to be happy about. Nothing could change the way she felt.

She turned dejectedly toward the basti. But her feet suddenly felt heavy. What if her friends yelled at her? What if they hadn't forgiven her yet for what happened to Mohan? Had any others been on the receiving end of violence the way Mohan was? Anjali closed her eyes, took a breath, and entered the basti.

Caked in splotches of color, Paro, Seema, and Rohit were drawing numbers in the dirt. But as soon as Anjali entered the colony, Paro's face lit up.

"Happy Holi!" she grinned, waving from beneath a layer of rainbow-colored powder matted into her skin.

"Happy Holi," said Anjali, forcing a smile, surprised at Paro's cheerful greeting. She crouched by the children. "I was worried about you. After what happened to Mohan—are you guys okay?"

Paro nodded. "I miss him."

"Where did he go?"

"No one knows," said Urmila.

Suraj nodded. "He just said he was never coming back."

Anjali pulled anxiously at her lip. She wanted desperately to know that Mohan was okay, and that the same fate wouldn't fall on Paro or any of the children if they came to school. Tears began spilling down her face and plopping into the dry earth. "I'm so sorry. I never meant for it to happen."

Paro put her hand on Anjali's hand. "Don't cry. Please." She squeezed then let go. "Wait here."

Anjali sniffled as Paro disappeared around the corner and came back with a small methi plant, its soil housed in old newspaper that had been folded into a little pot. She handed it to Anjali.

"For me?" asked Anjali.

Paro nodded. "Your Holi present."

Anjali ran her finger along one of the methi leaves. People didn't normally give presents at Holi. "But I didn't get you anything."

Paro shrugged. "That's okay."

Anjali smiled. This time, though, she wasn't pretending. She held on tightly to the little plant. "Thank you."

"The holiday must be hard with your mother gone," said a familiar voice near a hut.

Anjali turned in shock. It was Masterji.

"You didn't go to Indore?"

He shook his head. "Just for a little bit. But then our friends here were kind enough to let me hide here until things cooled down."

"Have they?" Anjali stopped, not wanting to say more in front of little Paro. Would Masterji be able to allow the integration to continue if he was hiding for his life? Or would there be a new teacher who wouldn't be so open to the idea?

Masterji nodded. "Everything's okay. They've moved on."

Anjali inhaled the fresh spring air, suddenly standing taller. It was going to be okay. Masterji would make sure the school was integrated. "But the school," she said softly, remembering that everything was not okay.

"I know," said Masterji. "New benches and tables are being been built. And the door will be repaired. It will take a few days, though."

Anjali couldn't stand it. More days without school. Without normalcy. Without a chance for the Dalit children to gain an education like everyone else.

She looked out past the road, catching sight of the hill that Pragati stood on. And the massive peepal tree—the sacred tree her mother used to always pause by. "You can see the school right there . . ." She trailed off.

Masterji chuckled. "Yes. I suppose I was hiding in plain sight. The charges were absurd, though, and as predicted, they soon forgot about me with all the real criminals they needed to arrest after these riots."

But Anjali had stopped listening. She couldn't stop staring at the peepal tree swaying in the evening breeze.

"I know how we can integrate the school," she said, turning to Masterji. "We can have class under Pragati's peepal tree. Just like Ma used to. On school property, for everyone, tomorrow. Even if the school is closed. And no one will be sitting in the back."

Masterji beamed at her. "Look at that. Enlightened without even meditating."

CHAPTER 30

As the sun dipped near the horizon, Anjali ran home, excited to tell her father all about her idea to keep her mother's work alive. The methi plant tickled her nostrils as she rounded the corner, inhaling its bitter but comforting aroma. She opened the gate to her compound, rushing to the porch, where Baba and Chachaji were talking. Behind them, Jamuna was using the long wooden stick to remove clothes from the clothesline.

"Look what Paro gave me. Can you make paratha with this?" Anjali asked Jamuna, her mouth watering at the thought of the spicy round flats of bread with a tinge of bitter methi.

Jamuna was about to reach for it when Chachaji intervened, swatting at the plant with his newspaper. "Chee! Put it away. I won't eat anything that's in. It'll be tainted."

"Chachaji," said Baba, gently putting the plant down, "it's perfectly good methi. Nobody's touch can taint anything. You have to let these superstitions go. They're wrong."

Anjali plucked a leaf off the plant in Baba's hand and chewed on it. Despite the bitter taste, she couldn't help but grin at how uncomfortable she was making Chachaji with her display.

Baba gave Anjali's braid a playful tug. "How about we go check on Nandini?" he asked, setting the plant down. "She's been acting a little restless this evening. I think the calf will be coming soon."

"Just watch," Chachaji said, following Baba and Anjali down the porch steps and to the backyard, "if you don't control her now, she'll turn into her mother. She has already brought disgrace to the family. Next step? Anjali will be wasting her life in jail."

"It would be an honor to go to jail for the freedom fight, Chachaji. I'm not afraid anymore." She turned to her father. "Baba, I know how to continue Ma's work even with the school closed. Tomorrow we're going to hold classes under the peepal tree—"

Anjali stopped. Inside the cow shed, Nandini was pacing back and forth, knocking her head against the short walls, agitated.

"Help her, Baba," Anjali pleaded as she watched Nandini slam her head so hard against one of the wooden pillars, the roof shook. They had to make sure Nandini was okay. They had to make sure she didn't lose another calf.

Baba patted Anjali on the head. "She'll be fine."

But Nandini didn't look fine. Her sides were trembling. Her breath was no longer warm. Her eyes looked like pits of agony as she kicked at her belly, her tail fully extended. Anjali saw her father and Chachaji exchange a look as they whispered between themselves.

Anjali could just make out one of Baba's sentences. "She's not progressing."

"The tail shouldn't be like that," Chachaji replied. "Something's wrong."

Something was wrong? Just like last time Nandini was pregnant? Anjali felt sick to her stomach. Nandini lay down, then stood up, then almost immediately lay down again, and then abruptly rose to her feet. Her legs wobbled so much she lost her balance, collapsing on the ground once more. Her eyes widened, panicked, and tears streamed down her white cheeks, staining them.

"She needs help," Chachaji said, his voice trembling.

Anjali thought of all the times Nandini had comforted her, all the times the gentle cow had wept, feeling Anjali's pain. And before Anjali knew what was happening, she too began to cry.

"Irfaan," she mumbled through her tears.

"What?" asked her father as he stroked the suffering cow's hide, looking helpless.

"We need them. They know about cows," she sobbed, backing away as Nandini wailed.

"I don't know if that's the best idea," replied her father.

But Anjali just ran.

"Anjali!" shouted Chachaji. "It's not safe for a little girl to—"

Anjali heard nothing. As warm tears trickled down her neck, she felt like she was drowning in Nandini's pain. Her sandals pounded the rocky ground below as she raced out the iron gate.

She sped around the bend, past families out celebrating Holi, and into an alley. A cockroach scrambled around her toes, but Anjali didn't even care. She ran and ran, pressure building in her chest, wheezing for breath. She wove around the few Muslim men sitting by their food stalls, briefly catching their words:

"Why do they have to celebrate so loudly?"

"Come now. Don't we do the same at Eid?"

Anjali's stomach tightened at the mention of Eid, at the memory of celebrating holidays with Irfaan, exchanging gifts and eating meals together. Back then, *she* didn't mind the Muslim celebration. She sprinted down a path and came to a stop at Irfaan's father's dairy.

"Farhan Uncle!" she screamed.

A group of boisterous men and woman danced nearby, banging their drums. The sound was deafening—Anjali had to be louder.

"Farhan Uncle!" she wailed, so loud her throat stung.

The door to Irfaan's home opened and Farhan Uncle came running out. "What is it, Anjali? What happened, beta? Why are you crying?"

From the doorframe, Irfaan watched sulkily.

"It's Nandini," Anjali got out, gasping for air. "She's dying."

Just like that, Irfaan's face changed. "Come on, Abbu," he begged his father, all signs of his venomous hate missing. "Now!"

CHAPTER 31

*A*njali, her father, Chachaji, and Irfaan stood outside the shed, waiting. Farhan Uncle emerged, smudges of crimson on his kurta visible in the evening light.

"We need methi," he said to Anjali's father, a worried crease on his forehead.

"Is that blood?" asked Anjali, focused on the kurta.

"Let's wait inside," suggested Irfaan. But Anjali wouldn't budge.

"Is that Nandini's blood?" she repeated, louder.

"It is, beta," responded Farhan Uncle. "Now, it's very important I get some methi. It's urgent."

Baba shook his head. "Our plants died."

Chachaji rushed to the front yard.

"And no market is open right now—"

Chachaji held up the methi plant from Paro in his wrinkled hand, out of breath from his run.

Anjali looked up at him in shock. "Chachaji?"

"It's perfectly good methi. Nandini needs it."

Anjali fell gratefully at Chachaji's feet, bowing to him. Chachaji put his hands around her, helping her back up, nodding to Anjali that everything was all right.

Irfaan gently touched Anjali's arm. "Let's go wait on the front porch."

Anjali and Irfaan walked around the compound and took a seat on the cool porch floor as the moon peeked out from behind a cloud.

Irfaan put his head on his knee, a sad look on his face. "I heard about what happened to your mother." He didn't continue, and Anjali didn't know what to say, since Irfaan's own mother had died years ago.

After a few moments, Anjali gave him a small smile. "You think anyone got Suman with some color this year?"

"I hope so," said Irfaan, digging his sandal into the small gaps between the steps.

Anjali pulled at the small patches of clover growing

to the side of the steps. Despite everything that had been said in the last few weeks between the two of them, deep down he was still the same old Irfaan. He was still her best friend, her brother, no matter what.

Just then a handful of dirt went flying at Anjali's face.

"Hey! What was that for?" shrieked Anjali, spitting out the grains.

Irfaan shrugged. "I didn't see any colored powder here."

Anjali grinned and chucked a handful of dirt at Irfaan.

Soon they were in a full-blown dirt fight as clumps of earth showered the air and their clothes.

Irfaan bent over, resting his hands on his knees as he caught his breath. "Okay, okay. I give up!"

Anjali dropped the rest of the dirt in her fist.

"Is there any badam barfi?" asked Irfan, still panting for air.

Anjali shook her head. "No. But I can have Jamuna make you some for tomorrow." She paused. "Greedy goat."

Irfaan beamed. "You know, it's been a long time since I've been called that."

"Anjali!" Baba's voice echoed in the night, despite the rolling drumbeats and hoots from the celebrations that were still going on outside.

"Nandini!" breathed Anjali. She raced to the cow shed, Irfaan right behind her.

Farhan Uncle stood by the shed's entrance with Anjali's father and Chachaji, his kurta stained even darker with maroon blood.

"Is she . . . ?" Anjali stopped, unable to finish the thought, her legs shaking unsteadily.

"Go in the shed," replied Anjali's father. "Both of you."

Anjali swallowed hard. She exchanged a nervous glance with Irfaan, and the two of them hesitantly entered the little shack.

There, glowing in the lantern light, was Nandini, sprawled sideways in the straw, breathing heavily as she weakly licked a tiny tan calf with deerlike eyes and a little wet black nose.

"You're okay," whispered Anjali as her gaze left Nandini and fell on the precious calf, whose ears twitched every time Nandini's chin grazed them.

"They're both okay," said Farhan Uncle, peeping inside. "I was able to turn the calf so she could come out. Now there's just one thing left to do."

Anjali furrowed her brow, wondering what he meant.

"Name the calf," Farhan Uncle said.

Without a moment's pause, Anjali looked at Irfaan and said, "Ahimsa."

Farhan Uncle nodded. "Ahimsa it is."

CHAPTER 32

The next morning, Ahimsa still hobbled occasionally, thanks to her shaky newborn knees, but she
was growing stronger by the hour. And Nandini was
recovering well. Following their custom, Jamuna
would make sure Ahimsa drank her fill before gently
milking Nandini for the family's portion.

Despite all the excitement last night and how tired
they were, Anjali and her father had still managed
to to help Masterji inform the other students that
school would be starting again today. It had been an
awkward moment at Suman's house when Lakshmi
Auntie opened the door and barked at Anjali to get off
her porch, but Anjali was still able to get the message
across, and saw Suman listening down the hall, even

if she said she wouldn't come. In fact, most of the parents had politely thanked Anjali and her father for the information but made it clear their children would not be coming to school.

Anjali tried to convince herself it didn't matter. She was keeping her promise to her mother. She had done her part in filling the pool with milk. Now it was up to everyone else to decide for themselves.

Anjali petted the calf on the head and headed out with her father by her side. She smiled at him, certain today would be the start of a new era. Nothing could bring her down. After all, today was finally the day that Suraj, Dinanath, Kavita, Jyoti, Seema, Rohit, Vijay, Urmila, and Paro would get to go to school with Anjali and Irfaan. She couldn't wait to visit her mother in prison and tell her all about this historic day for their segregated neighborhood.

As she neared the peepal tree outside Pragati, Anjali spotted Masterji sitting in its shade. Paro and the eight other young children from the basti were sitting cross-legged in a circle in the dusty dirt around the tree, staring intently at the small chalkboard Masterji held.

Masterji had already started, and was writing math

problems on it that the children were copying onto their donated notebooks. Irfaan, sitting next to Paro, waved when he saw Anjali.

She took her seat on the other side of Paro and took out her notebook too. Anjali copied the numbers down, but she couldn't help but feel a little uncomfortable. It wasn't from the rugged ground she was sitting on. Sure, they were on school property. Dalit children were on school property, learning in full view of the world, and not forced to sit in the back of the classroom like second-class citizens. But without any of the other students here, it really didn't feel like everyone was a part of Pragati. It didn't feel like this was any different from just learning outside in their basti. It didn't feel like any of her absent classmates and neighbors would ever change.

Anjali ran her fingers through the thin grass near her spot in the circle, twisting the blades with her left hand as she wrote with her right. Where were the others? How could this have happened? Was this what Mohan meant when he said she was like that horse with blinders on? She couldn't help but feel like she had failed her mother. Like her mother's dream could never be a reality. And if that were true, did that mean the dream of an India full of equals who could stand strong, united against the British, would also never come true?

She erased the numbers in her notebook. This whole setup was like something written in lead. Quick to disappear. Not permanent. And not important if it didn't help change anyone else's mind.

"Shame on you," muttered the vegetable vendor bitterly as he stopped his cart by the school.

Paro flinched as the crabby old man splattered some of the water from the container on his cart in the children's direction, falling short of his target.

Masterji stopped writing. "Have these children done anything to you?"

The vendor glared. "Yes. They've scared away my business."

"The riots scared away your business," said Anjali bitterly. "Now if you don't mind, we're trying to hold class here."

The grocer grumbled under his breath as he shoved his cart forward, looking for customers.

"Don't worry about him," said Anjali to Paro. "No one will hurt you here." She paused, thinking of Mohan. Could she really promise such a thing? Could she really ensure that Paro would be safe? The little girl looked scared.

Anjali felt awful. Nothing was changing. This was pointless. Worse, this was hopeless. She and Irfaan were the only original Pragati students in this class. How could the course of history be changed when nothing was actually changing for the Dalit children in this outdoor class? And no other students' views on the caste system were being changed, either?

Anjali erased everything on her page even harder, trying not to show her frustration in front of the other kids. Then a girl's shadow fell on her notepad.

It was Suman.

Anjali glared at Suman. "Are you here to tell me how this is ruining your ranking?"

Suman sat down and took out her notebook and pencil. "I'm here to make sure I keep my ranking."

Anjali stopped erasing so suddenly, her page tore.

"I want to learn." Suman gave Anjali a quick glance as she continued to write down the lesson. "And so do they."

Anjali scanned the street, just over the hill. Nirmala, Anasuya, and four other students from her class were slowly approaching the school. They looked unsure and a little scared, but soon they too sat down with Anjali, Irfaan, and the other children.

Suman shrugged. "What good is being number one in a class full of kids who have never been to school before? That just didn't seem fair. So I told them to come."

It was strange logic, but it meant seven old students in addition to Irfaan and Anjali were in their class. It meant nine Dalit children were now in a class with kids from every other caste, sitting side by side as equals.

It meant things were finally changing.

Maybe everything wasn't so hopeless after all.

CHAPTER 33

*L*ater that March afternoon, as the sun began to set, Anjali was a bundle of excitement. Her father was going to take her to the prison to see Ma. And though it was the eighteenth day of her mother's fast, and she wasn't sure how her mother would look, Anjali couldn't wait to tell her everything—integrating the school today, Nandini's calf being born, everything.

She and Irfaan were playing with the new calf, waiting for Anjali's father to return with word they had permission to head to the prison, when the familiar patriotic cry of "Jai Hind" was heard down the street.

A crowd of khadi-clad protesters marched by the

bungalow, their fists raised forcefully, some holding blazing torches. All the joy from the previous day's Holi celebrations had gone.

Beads of sweat made their way down Irfaan's worried face. "A protest? Another riot?"

Anjali sprang to her feet and headed for the iron gate with a nervous Irfaan in tow. Her father would be home any minute now, and they needed to get to the prison. She needed to see her mother. "Come on."

There must have been hundreds of people protesting. She recognized Balkishan and other freedom fighters from the Khadi Shop meetings. They were all dressed in white. But there were others there too. Others who looked like they had just been walking on the street and decided to join in.

"Jai Hind!" yelled Anjali, raising her fist. She shrugged to Irfaan. "I can tell my mother I not only helped the school become integrated today, I also joined a protest."

"Anjali," he hissed, "it's not a protest. It's a funeral."

Anjali came to a sudden stop, almost getting crushed by the marchers behind her. "What?"

Irfaan pointed up in front of them. A lifeless body

was being carried on a platform, wrapped in white. Anjali rushed forward. She had to get a glimpse. She had to see who had died. She had to—

"Keshavji?" Anjali said, feeling dizzy. She stepped out of the procession, Irfaan right behind her. If Keshavji was dead, did it mean her mother—

"Anjali!" her father screamed, pushing his way through the crowd to her side. "What are you two doing out here?"

"Keshavji!" replied Anjali. "He's dead."

Anjali's father nodded. "I just heard when I met the lawyers. It happened this morning. He tried to escape, and . . ."

"Why would Keshavji have tried to escape? He was so positive. So sure freedom was coming."

"Some people are saying the police made it up. They just needed an excuse to get rid of him before he could stir people up against the British again."

"What about Ma?"

Baba bent down to her level. "She's fine. Absolutely fine. I promise. But with everything that happened, they aren't letting us see her today."

Anjali's face fell.

"How about we pay Keshavji our respects? The

procession will pass the Khadi Shop on the way to the riverbank for the cremation."

That was almost a one-and-a-half-mile walk. But Anjali nodded. "Ma would want us to." She squeezed her father's hand and walked forward with Irfaan. As devastating as it was that Keshavji was no longer amongst the living, Anjali couldn't help but feel massive amounts of relief at the fact that her mother was safe.

Anjali and Irfaan stuck close to Baba as they neared the basti. Paro's grandmother was standing on the side of the street talking to three men from the basti. Anjali watched as they too joined the group. The procession passed Captain Brent's bungalow. Anjali scanned his yard, but there was no sign of him. He must have been inside lounging on his sofa and enjoying some tea, Anjali thought as they rounded tiny shops selling books and tea stalls, passed the temple, and walked into the business district toward the cremation site along the riverbank. With each building they passed, the group gained marchers.

Anjali's feet were beginning to swell from the distance. They had been walking so long the sun was just barely visible, having painted the sky with strokes of peach and orange. She looked back through the crowd, spotting Paro's grandmother. Anjali's thighs ached, but if an old woman could keep up, she reasoned that she should too, so she kept pushing forward. She wanted to help escort Keshavji one last time to the Khadi Shop he had helped build. To the spot where he had inspired so many. To the place that meant so much to Ma.

As Anjali walked, she studied the faces around her. They were angry, hopeful, distressed—every single face seemed to be expressing a different hue of emotion, and Anjali wondered what her own face was giving away.

The mass of people turned the bend and entered the narrow streets in the business district. It was getting cramped, and Anjali and Irfaan were getting pushed from all sides. Baba put his arms around them protectively.

The funeral procession came to a stop just outside the Khadi Shop. Several Indian policemen were blocking the entrance to the building, rifles—instead of lathis—raised to the sky.

Captain Brent, standing behind two armed British policemen, shouted orders to the crowd. "Stop where you are! Mr. Parmar's death is a pity, but it was the result of someone tampering with the law. We understand your grief, but we cannot allow you to bring the procession this way and incite more violence!" Beads of nervous perspiration danced down his red cheeks. "Effective immediately, this store is being shut down. The emotions it elicits are just too much. We've had enough violence in this town."

"This is unacceptable!" shouted a fiery young man. "We want you out! Quit India!"

With that, a roar went up in the crowd. Anjali didn't feel inspired, though—she felt scared. There was an unfamiliar anger to the shouts, a strange fire burning in the marchers' eyes. It was everything *but* ahimsa.

Before she could give it a second thought, though, she was forced forward as a surge of people in the crowd furiously stormed the Khadi Shop. Baba and Irfaan were being shoved forward with her in separate directions. Anjali screamed as her body was pinned on all sides, crumpling between the sweaty bodies of the mob.

Warning shots from the police were fired in the air.

"Kids! Get down!" screeched Anjali's father from a few people away.

"How?" asked Anjali. She was being shoved left and right by the sprinting protesters, and before she knew it, she, Irfaan, and her father were almost face-to-face with the two British policemen.

A rock whizzed by her face, just missing her ear as it pelted a lanky white officer to Captain Brent's right. A trickle of deep crimson blood slunk down the man's face, making Anjali feel faint. Suddenly more rocks were launched. Anjali's father bent his body over Anjali and Irfaan, shielding them. Desperate people clambered by her, unaware that their chains and rings scraped her flesh as they passed. Anjali saw a flash of metal, and she instantly knew what it was. Someone had brought a knife.

She heard a terrible gushing sound as the blade entered flesh. A mustached Indian policeman fell to the ground, his thigh bleeding as a young man with the knife disappeared into the crowd. Another policeman whipped his rifle against the forehead of an old man, knocking him to the ground. Anjali just stared at his boat-shaped hat lying on the ground. She was too scared to glance at the man himself.

In a second, she wouldn't have been able to spot him even if she had tried. More people charged at the officers, angry, frustrated, lashing out. All around them, blood was flowing, fiery torches were swinging, rocks were flying, and people were dropping. Freedom fighters, policemen . . . the screams of the wounded and the attackers mixed in the air as the coppery smell of fresh blood invaded Anjali's nostrils.

She peered through the limbs and caught a glimpse of Paro's grandmother being led away from the crowd by the other men from the basti. Anjali breathed easier, but then she saw familiar faces from the meetings, faces that had gone along with every nonviolent thing Keshavji had preached, now twisted in frustrated fury. Balkishan and a small mob were in the process of wrestling the bloodied British policeman's rifle out of his grip. Captain Brent's and the remaining British officer's guns were no longer aimed at the sky. They were aimed right at the mob. The mob Anjali was trapped in.

This was how Nirmala's uncle died, thought Anjali, shaking. *This is how I'm going to die.*

A shot cracked out of the muzzle of the white officer's rifle. Then another. And another.

A man screamed.

"Baba?" Anjali whimpered, afraid to turn around.

But her father was still there, still standing. He

firmly put his hands on her cheeks, forcing her head forward, stopping her from turning. Stopping her from seeing. But she could still hear.

She could hear the tormented, anguished screams of a man with a bullet lodged in his body. It was terrifying, but Anjali pried her father's hands off her head and turned to the sight.

A young man in his twenties writhed unnaturally on the ground, blood trickling down his hip, saturating the white khadi cloth of his pants.

"It's on fire!" shouted a voice from deep within the sea of people.

Anjali looked back. Just a few feet away, flames were shooting out of the third story of the Khadi Shop. The floor that housed all the wooden spinning wheels and looms. The floor where Ma taught new members of the freedom fight to make homespun clothes.

"No," Anjali gasped.

There was a bolt of action all around her, as the hundreds of Indians in the funeral procession turned on the police . . . and on Captain Brent.

A foot away from Anjali, Captain Brent's face turned paler than she thought his light skin could. Men from the crowd charged at him. He stumbled back, dropping his revolver as punches and kicks from unknown fists and feet pummeled him to the ground.

The flames in the Khadi Shop grew, spreading to the other floors. The crackling fire was spitting out surges of heat that were firing up the already-enraged crowd.

Anjali saw another knife glisten in the sun as it was raised by a tall Indian man with fury in his eyes. Captain Brent was going to die. She felt like the world was tilting, but something inside her made her stand tall, almost steady.

"No! We have to do this nonviolently!" she yelled, moving away from Baba, trying to get the crowd's attention as a couple men dragged an injured protestor out of the mayhem.

"Anjali, stay back," begged her father, trying to make his way to her.

But Anjali's feet moved before her brain had even made the decision. She rushed forward, ducking under the crowd and forcing back sweaty arms and fists, until she made her way to Captain Brent. He had collapsed, his face now battered, like Mohan's had been.

Anjali stood right in front of him. "Ahimsa!" she cried.

A foot flew past her, slamming into Captain Brent's gut. He moaned, slumping farther into the ground.

"Ahimsa . . ." Her voice was rocky.

Fists and sandals fought their way past her tiny blockade. One made contact with Anjali, striking her side. Anjali dropped to the ground, throwing her scrawny body over Captain Brent's bloated one. "Ahimsa!" she yelled amidst the chaos.

"Ahimsa!" called out another voice, even shakier than hers.

It was Irfaan. He took her hands in his and helped her to her feet. And there they stood, in front of Captain Brent, protecting him in a little circle.

"Ahimsa!" they shouted together.

It suddenly got quiet.

Anjali heard a knife fall to the ground. The crowd backed away, dropping their weapons and folding their hands in namaste, asking Captain Brent for forgiveness. Balkishan sobbed into his bruised hands, ashamed.

A hand opened toward Captain Brent and pulled him to his feet. "Forgive us, brother." It was Anjali's father.

Captain Brent looked at Anjali, and she saw

something transform in his eyes. It wasn't a look of contempt. It wasn't even a look of gratitude.

It was a look of respect.

He trembled, quickly looking down, seemingly shocked to be alive, unable to make eye contact with the Indians bowing their heads before him.

Anjali couldn't, either. She was too busy staring at the sight of the Khadi Shop gone up in flames. Its light blue paint was being charred black as the scent of the burning wooden looms and spinning wheels filled the air. As the last rays of the evening sun faded away, thick black smoke spewed from the shop's windows as hundreds and hundreds of homespun clothes made with the thread spun by Ma, Keshavji, and so many others burned away to nothing but ash.

CHAPTER 34

*T*hat night, an exhausted Anjali sat on her bed as Jamuna applied turmeric to her scrapes and cuts. "I'm okay," she said, flinching at Jamuna's touch.

"Does it hurt?"

"No." Anjali winced as Jamuna smeared the turmeric a little too roughly into a long cut on her arm. Anjali gripped her bed and felt something poking out. It was her saffron ghagra-choli, her gorgeous Diwali present from two years ago that she had tucked away under her mattress when she was desperate to save it from being burned by her mother.

Her mother.

Anjali ran her fingers over the ghagra underneath her, and tears spilled down her cheeks. She missed

Ma. She was so worried for her. Worried that she too might end up dead like Keshavji, either at the hands of a guard or from her fast that had now been going on for more than two weeks.

Jamuna held her, trying in vain to comfort her, but it made Anjali feel even worse. It should've been her mother holding her, stroking her hair. Instead, her mother was in jail. She was wasting away there, and Anjali couldn't even visit her to tell her about the joys of succeeding in getting Paro into school or the horror of the Khadi Shop burning down.

Just then, there was a loud knock at the front door. Anjali wiped at her tears. They weren't expecting company. She peeked into the hall as her father opened the door.

Baba turned to Anjali, stunned. "It's for you. It's . . . It's Brent Sahib."

Captain Brent entered the house, his face swollen and purple from his attack earlier that day. Awkwardly, he approached Anjali, his eyes downcast.

It was hard for her to maintain eye contact too. A British officer was in her house. She didn't know what to think.

Captain Brent handed her a piece of paper.

"What is this?" she asked, scanning the big English words.

"The letter. The pardon letter you asked me for. Requesting leniency for your mother."

The paper shivered in her hand. "Are you doing this because of what happened today?"

Captain Brent shook his head. "I'm doing this because it's right."

Anjali couldn't believe it. This letter was going to change everything. It was going to finally make all of her pain go away.

She ran into Baba's arms. It was all over. Ma was going to be okay. She turned to Captain Brent. "Thank you."

He nodded. "I'll let myself out," he said, heading for the door with a slight limp. "Nobody likes cockroaches in their own house, right?"

Anjali clenched the letter tightly as Captain Brent hobbled out.

CHAPTER 35

The next day, the sound of gold bangles jingling melodiously against one another filled the early morning air as Anjali moved a paintbrush in a horizontal line, staining the wood in front of her. Kneeling in the grass, she was painting the replacement sign for Pragati onto a newly cut little wooden arch to go above the door. Her arm was sore but okay, her cuts now healing, her bruises her temporary reminder of a day filled with the highest of highs and the lowest of lows.

"My turn!" said Paro, crouching beside her. She painted the Hindi letters for Pragati under the line Anjali had made.

"It's perfect." Irfaan beamed, admiring the work

as Masterji and Farhan Uncle passed them, carrying wooden benches into the school.

At the bottom of the hill by the road, a rickshaw came to a stop. Baba was sitting in it.

Anjali tapped Irfaan on the arm. "He's here," she said, waving to her friends as she ran down the hill.

"Are we all set? Can we go?" she asked, taking a seat next to her father on the rickshaw.

Baba held Captain Brent's letter. "Nothing can stop us."

They zipped through the streets, the rickshawalla pedaling with his lean, muscular legs. Everything seemed to be back to normal. Dogs played in the dust. Groups of women sang and danced in the alleys. Old men happily shined their store windows.

Anjali took in the sights but wished they would go by quicker, wished the rickshawalla would pedal faster. That would mean they were almost there.

They rounded a tree-lined street and turned once more. Then the rickshaw pulled to a stop.

"We're here," announced Baba, helping Anjali out of the carriage and paying their fare.

They were finally here. At the prison.

Anjali ran through the dilapidated building. She

whizzed by the other prisoners, skirted past the solemn guards around every corner, rushed through the courtyard, entered the women's prison, and came to a sudden stop in front of a cell.

A lone guard was in the process of unlocking it. Anjali's mother was finally going to be released.

"Ma!" cried Anjali as her father caught up to them.

Her mother, reduced to almost nothing, was resting against the bars.

"Did you hear, Ma? Paro and Kavita, Urmila, Suraj, Vijay, Dinanath, Jyoti, Seema, and Rohit . . . we were all in school together yesterday, Ma. Even Suman."

Anjali paused, thinking of Mohan, wishing he had been able to be there alongside her other classmates.

But Ma's eyes, dull from weeks of fasting, suddenly brightened.

And Anjali felt her heart flutter with hope. Things could change. Things had changed. At one point she thought she would never see Ma again and here they were, face to face. Maybe one day she would see Mohan again.

"It happened. It finally happened. And this is just the start. When you're up to it, Baba and I thought we could help distribute more charkhas to the villages. In honor of Keshavji."

Ma looked proudly at her daughter. "Jai Hind," she said with what little voice she had left.

Anjali nodded. "Jai Hind."

There was a heavy sound of metal hitting metal as the guard opened the cell door. Anjali threw herself into her mother's embrace as tears trickled down both their faces.

Baba put his arm around his wife, gently supporting her weak frame. "Shall we?"

Anjali took a deep breath as she grasped her mother's hand. The smoke from the past few months of hatred and violence had cleared, and the winds were blowing fresh air their way. As she helped her mother take her first feeble steps outside the prison, something shimmered on the ground before them.

It was a peacock feather.

After all these months, a feather.

Anjali stepped over it, clinging harder to her mother's hand, and smiled. She didn't need any superstitions to make her feel better today. Freedom was in the air.

ACKNOWLEDGMENTS

I started working on *Ahimsa* fourteen years and many drafts ago. I am indebted to those who have helped me along this journey.

To Aai and Dad, I can't thank you enough for encouraging me to follow my dream. Your support and sacrifice have allowed me to get to where I am today, and I am eternally grateful.

To Sachit, thank you for the countless library runs, for dedicating your vacations to my writing, and for being the staunchest believer in my success.

To Arjun, Leykh, and Zuey, thanks for the entertainment and for occasionally sleeping.

To Apoorva, Baiju, Aashish, and my mother-in-law and father-in-law for the encouragement.

To Cookie and Limca, who took turns sitting by my side from the beginning to the end of this project.

To Sandhya Mami and Dilip Mama for filling my world with books. To my niece, Kaia, for being *Ahimsa*'s first reader. To my parents and Nalini Verma, Chandu Sarwate, Vilas Kale, Suman Joshi, Professor Madhav Deshpande, and Adil Daudi for the answers to my many questions.

To Brynn, who has read almost everything I've written since middle school, thank you for always knowing just what to say. And to two of the best writers I know, Andrea and Dave Turner, for almost two decades of critique notes and friendship.

To the kid lit community, including the wonderful Axie Oh, the #2017Debuts and #TeamKRush for all the help navigating this new world. And to Sangeeta Mehta for her insight.

To the two people who have influenced my writing the most. Jim Burnstein, who I was so lucky to learn from at the University of Michigan. And Vidhu Vinod Chopra, thank you for rescuing that paper from the trash sixteen years ago. You changed my life.

To the smartest agent to have in your corner, Kathleen

Rushall. Thank you for your help, guidance, and for always cheering me on.

To Mimi Mondal for her perspective on the Dalit community. To *Ahimsa*'s designer, Neil Swaab, and cover artist Kate Forrester for the absolutely stunning cover. To copy editor Shveta Thakrar, marketing director Hannah Ehrlich, Keilin Huang, Jalissa Corrie, the New Visions Award selection committee, and the entire team at Tu Books and Lee & Low Books for making this book what it is today.

To my editor and publisher, Stacy Whitman, for championing the underrepresented voice, for shaping my words, and for making my dream come true. Thank you for believing in this book. It has been a total joy and privilege to get to work with you and learn from you.

And finally, a huge thanks to my friends and family who have been there for me through it all. There are too many of you to name, and it isn't lost on me how very lucky that makes me. I love you all dearly, and none of this would have been possible without you by my side.

AUTHOR'S NOTE

Anjali's story takes place in the fictional town of Navrangpur, a Hindi-speaking town I envisioned two hundred miles northeast of what is now known as Mumbai. India is a large, diverse country with twenty-three official languages and hundreds of dialects, written in several different scripts. The Indian words used in this novel are Hindi. Along with the many languages spoken in India, there are a multitude of cultural practices and experiences that can vary from region to region and family to family. So while many of the moments described in this book were experienced by my family members, they may differ from the experiences of another person from a different part of India.

Although this story is fictional, several of the events and concepts mentioned in it are not.

The British first came to control parts of India in the 1700s, under the East India Company. However, in 1858, control of the East India Company's majority of India was transferred over to the British Crown, or "the Raj," as it was commonly referred to in the Indian subcontinent.

Mohandas K. Gandhi, also known as Mahatma Gandhi, began his civil disobedience campaign against the British in the early 1900s in South Africa, and later became one of the most influential leaders of the independence movement in India through various methods of passive resistance.

The spinning wheel mentioned in this book was one such method. By getting Indians to go back to the use of the spinning wheel, Gandhi felt the village economy could be boosted. If villagers once again spun cotton rather than the industrial mills, which had become the norm under British rule, then the sizing, dyeing, and weaving industries would also be sustained. The ability to be self-reliant could help India break free from the Raj as well.

Gandhi burned foreign-spun clothes decades before

this story takes place, but he later regretted it, writing that he had been "burning cloth utterly regardless of the fact that [the famine-stricken at Khulna] were dying of hunger and nakedness."

Gandhi used to spin fiber into thread every day in his ashram. In fact, the spinning wheel had so much importance as a symbol of Indian self-sufficiency that an earlier, pre-Independence version of the Indian flag had the spinning wheel in the center of it. This spinning wheel was later changed to a multispoked wheel representing the wheel of dharma, also called the wheel of Ashoka, an ancient Buddhist emperor who ruled over the majority of the Indian subcontinent and renounced violence. But even though the spinning wheel is no longer on the Indian flag, by law, the flag must be made of hand-spun or hand-woven wool, cotton, or silk khadi.

In addition to the khadi movement, Gandhi had many other innovative ways of dealing with the British. He protested the British tax on Indian salt by leading a two-hundred-forty-one-mile march to the Arabian sea over twenty-two days to grab a handful of salt from the banks, and fasted several times for various reasons, including in protest of Hindu-Muslim violence. Gandhi often emptied waste from toilets and made all new inhabitants at his ashrams remove the waste from the dry toilets and bury it in pits.

Gandhi left the Indian Congress Party a few years before World War II to work on helping the poor. When World War II broke out, though, some Indian leaders thought it was an opportune time to heighten the effort for India's independence. Gandhi once again returned to the fight and helped start the Quit India movement in 1942. In response, the British government imprisoned him and most of the Indian Congress. By 1945, things began to change, and the negotiations for India's independence began. The centuries-long hard work of the freedom fighters had finally paid off, and on August 15, 1947, India finally gained its independence.

India is now the world's largest democracy, but its independence came at a cost to the people, as the subcontinent was divided into two nations when the British agreed to leave: India and Pakistan. The division led to a violent start to two nations, with Hindus and Muslims fleeing in both directions across the border between India and Pakistan. In 1948, Gandhi was assassinated by Nathuram Godse, who felt that

Gandhi was partially responsible for splitting India and allowing the creation of Pakistan.

The Hindu caste system mentioned in this novel was designed thousands of years ago to classify the population into four categories. At the top was the Brahmin, or scholarly caste, some of whom were priests, to which Anjali's family belonged. Next was the warrior caste, then the caste consisting of traders and other landowners, and then the laborer caste. Those who weren't categorized into these four groups formed a fifth caste, the Dalits. Although the caste system was constitutionally abolished in 1950, many people still face discrimination and hardship due to the stigmas associated with their caste.

While not all freedom fighters were social reformers, some did believe there was a dual struggle: an internal one, battling the social injustices in India, and an external one, against the British—because when independence was eventually gained, the country's social problems had to be solved. In this story, burning clothes and making khadi is part of Ma's contribution to fighting against the British, while helping all Indians in her community become equal was part of her contribution to India's homegrown issues.

For other freedom fighters, social causes (including Dalit politics) and the politics of independence were considered separate entities. The movement to gain equal treatment for Dalits continued well after India gained its freedom from the British.

The fictional character of Keshavji lived at Gandhi's ashram, where many Dalits had lived. Although Gandhi is often portrayed as a saint, it is important to remember he was a real person who was not perfect, and who sometimes made racist, prejudicial statements we would never condone today. As such, many Dalits did not and do not agree with all of Gandhi's ideas or think he had their best interests in mind. They felt and feel that Gandhi wanted them to assimiliate, but Dr. Bhimrao Raji Ambedkar, also known as Dr. Babasaheb Ambedkar, wanted to emancipate them.

Dr. Ambedkar, the father of the Indian constitution, was a Dalit. His father served in the army, and Dr. Ambedkar was the only Dalit boy in his school. He had to sit by himself on the floor in the corner at school, and no one was allowed to talk to him. In his teens, he was the sole Dalit student at a government school. This time he was allowed to sit on the back bench. Once, a teacher asked him to solve a question on the chalkboard. That was where the upper caste children's lunch boxes were kept, and they rushed to grab their tiffin containers before the mere presence of Ambedkar could "pollute" them. The adversity continued into his later school years as well, when Ambedkar was not allowed to learn Sanskrit because it was the language of the Hindu texts. Despite these cruel hardships, Ambedkar continued to study, and in 1908 he went to college and then did his postgraduate work at Columbia University and got his Ph.D.

Dr. Ambedkar became a political leader and fought for the rights of "Depressed Classes." In 1938 he walked out in protest of the Bombay Legislative Assembly when Congress accepted Gandhi's usage of "Harijan," which he considered condescending. Dr. Ambedkar renounced Hinduism because of the caste system, and he and millions of Dalits became Buddhists. Buddhism, a religion founded in ancient India, has no caste system. After independence in 1947, Dr. Ambedkar went on to become the Chairman of the Drafting Committee for the new constitution.

The Rani of Jhansi, the queen young Anjali made a drawing of, was a real queen who was seen as a symbol of rebellion against the British in the 1800s. Although there are conflicting reports as to how active she actually was in the fight, some historians agree that while initially she was forced by the Indian Sepoys to join their rebellion, later she fought the British on her own accord.

Decades later, in the 1940s, it wasn't uncommon for women to be involved in the freedom movement. The character of Shailaja is inspired by my great-grandmother, Anasuyabai Kale. She was a brave, determined woman who came from humble roots yet was able to contribute a lot to the freedom fight, all with the support of her progressive husband. Anasuyabai Kale worked with Mahatma Gandhi, was imprisoned for her civil disobedience, fought for women's rights, met with Dr. Ambedkar, and managed to get seven political prisoners—who were to be sent to the gallows—off death row. After independence, Anasuyabai Kale went on to become a two-term Congresswoman.

She, and all the Indians, young and old, male and female, who participated in the Gandhian movement for independence, proved that anyone can change the world for the better when they set their minds to it, and they can do it without violence. What a great testament to the power of ahimsa.

FURTHER READING

Gandhi: A March to the Sea

by Alice B. McGinty

Grandfather Gandhi

by Arun Gandhi and Bethany Hegedus

Be the Change: A Grandfather Gandhi Story

by Arun Gandhi and Bethany Hegedus

Columbia University's website on Dr. Ambedkar:

"Dr. B. R. Ambedkar who tried to turn the Wheel of the Law toward

social justice for all," by Frances W. Pritchett

columbia.edu/itc/mealac/pritchett/00ambedkar/index.html

GLOSSARY

ahimsa: Nonviolence, a tenet found in Indian religions like Jainism, Buddhism, and Hinduism. Mahatma Gandhi used the principal of ahimsa in his movement of civil disobedience against the British.

badam: Almonds.

basti: An area with low-income housing.

beta: Child.

chapati: Indian flatbread.

charkha: A wooden spinning wheel used by villagers to spin raw cotton into thread that could later be woven into fabric on a loom. The charkha became a symbol of the Gandhian movement. Charkhas could be upright or flat and compact, inside of a wooden box that opened flat, like a book.

gilli danda: Also called gulli danda, gilli danda is a common street game in India. The gilli is a small cylindrical stick that is narrowed down on both ends. The danda is a long stick that is used to flip the gilli out of a divot in the ground and bat the gilli.

Jai Hind: "Victory to India."

-ji: A Hindi and Urdu suffix added to names to show respect.

khadi: Homespun cotton, silk, or wool.

methi: The Hindi word for "fenugreek," methi is a nutrient-rich plant whose leaves and seeds are used in Indian cooking and for medicinal purposes.

namaste: A greeting made by placing your palms and fingers together as if in prayer.

paan: A food item made by stuffing a betel leaf with various ingredients like areca nut, fennel seed, anise seed, lime paste, rose jam, and coconut. It is folded into a triangle and eaten after meals.

paanwalla: A man who sells paan.

pranaam: Bowing down respectfully to your elders for their blessing.

salwar kameez/pajama kurta: An outfit worn by women and men in India. A salwar is a pair of pants. A kurta (*kur-thaa*), or kameez, is a long shirt that is usually knee-length, although the lengths of the kurta vary based on the style and season.